MURDER IN FANCY DRESS

Also by Laurie Mantell
A MURDER OR THREE

MURDER IN FANCY DRESS

LAURIE MANTELL

WALKER AND COMPANY
NEW YORK

First published in the United States of America in 1981 by the Walker Publishing Company, Inc.

Published simultaneously in Canada by John Wiley & Sons Canada Limited, Rexdale, Ontario

ISBN: 0-8027-5446-5

Library of Congress Catalog Card Number: 81-51971

Printed in the United States of America

10 9 8 7 6 5 4 3 2 1

MURDER IN FANCY DRESS

CHAPTER I

DETECTIVE SERGEANT Steven Arrow stood on the corner of the street, hands clasped loosely behind him. The sign at his feet said "To Virginia City" but no one would find Virginia City in the direction indicated.

A garish placard over the bus stop stated a stage coach left for Korokoro twice daily and, by the post office, a public notice requested citizens to leave their guns with the sheriff. Nearly every third person on the crowded pavement was wearing western costume.

Steven smiled to himself. Funny how things happened. Someone had been indiscreet enough to remark that Petone reminded him of an old cowtown in a bad TV programme.

Maybe he had a point. Petone was an old town—population 10,000—set on the northern shore of Wellington Harbour, New Zealand. One main street running parallel to the beach, shopping centre in the middle, a surround of residential area then factories running east to the Hutt River, west to the railway station at the foot of the Koro Koro Hills.

But Petone bred a fierce loyalty in its citizens. They were all ready to do battle when, fortunately, someone laughed, suggested the business section should take advantage of this adverse publicity by inviting everyone to celebrate Ponderosa Day.

The town hastily acquired a western look. Horse troughs appeared, hitching posts, bales of straw in every other doorway. Shop assistants dressed for the occasion: men in jeans, plaid shirts, bright bandannas; women in trim shirt waists, long skirts.

Prizes were offered lavishly, including a bounty of $200 to the person who guessed the identities of four outlaws scheduled to rob the bank at a quarter to two. Wanted posters everywhere

7

displayed photographs of 25 citizens, four of whom would be the outlaws.

The public lapped it up. They thronged the footpaths, chuckling over the town's transformation, crowing over exhibitions of old-time equipment, fashions, in shop windows.

Traffic crawled through Jackson Street, a situation that could have lent itself to frayed tempers, minor crashes, yet, strangely, the cars flowed smoothly, drivers thoroughly alert, delightedly amused.

The only obvious omissions were horses but they would be on stage when the shopping centre was closed to cars and the robbery took place.

"Why, hello, Steven. What are you doing here? I thought you were attached to Lower Hutt?"

Steven looked down into the kindly face of a small, dark-haired woman dressed in the fashion of a century ago.

"Reinforcements, Mrs Robinson. The bank's going to be robbed, remember?" He stepped back to view her dress. "Why, that's beautiful! Where'd you get hold of that?"

"Like it?" Mrs Robinson swirled the long skirts. "My great-grandmother's. Thought I'd get it out for the occasion."

"Good idea! You look really something." He admired the soft grey material, the intricately rucked bodice, the delicate blue of the formal muff. "You'll have to let Kylie see that."

"I'll call in on the way home. Has Kylie been down here yet? To see the window displays? Oh, Steven, there's an old spinning wheel in Warner's. And a christening gown over 100 years old at Clary's. Absolutely charming."

Steven nodded. "Yes, I brought her down at lunch time. Might be the only time she'll see anything like this."

Mrs Robinson smiled. "Probably. But it's fun, isn't it? Everyone's really entered into the spirit of the thing. Well, I'd better be on my way. Never get the messages done at this rate."

She walked swiftly away, long skirt held lightly in her mittened hand, seemingly unaware of admiring glances.

Steven wandered along the edge of the footpath, watching pedestrians coalesce into little knots at some exhibit, fan out again to proceed to the next novelty.

He stopped to read witticisms plastered over one of the hotels, renamed The Golden Horseshoe for the occasion. They were probably extremely clever but, being unfamiliar with local characters named, he failed to see the point of some.

He was about to move on when the sound of a shot sent him spinning round. Instinctively, his hand went out, grasped the pistol levelled at him.

The gun belonged to a moon-faced youngster dressed as a cowboy, star-studded band on his wide hat, silver spurs on his tooled boots.

Steven released his hold. "Sorry," he laughed. "Lost my head there for a moment. Thought you were trying to kill me."

"Did kill you. Did kill you. Lie down dead."

Steven started. "Come off it, fella! In this crowd! I'd be trampled to death." Hoping to divert attention, he bent over the boy. "My word, that's a beauty gun you've got there. A wheel-lock, isn't it?"

He took hold of the ancient weapon, fingers sliding over the walnut stock with its minutely-pierced and engraved steel inlay. A wheellock, all right. But it had not been fired. "How d'you make the pistol shot?" he asked casually.

The boy held out his other hand, opened to show a crumpled pack of throwdowns. "Well, careful with those," Steven advised. "Might frighten someone. Where'd you get the gun?"

"My father."

"And who's your father?"

"My father. My father."

For the first time, Steven looked directly at the boy, saw his eyes. Straightening, he searched the crowd for a helmeted head.

One of the local uniform men was leaning nonchalantly against a nearby shop window. Steven signalled.

Small fingers plucked at his hand. "My gun! Want my gun!"

"All right, fella. Here you are." He handed the gun back without relaxing his hold. "Does your father know you have it?"

The boy scowled. " 'Smine. 'Smine. Gimme." He tugged at the gun, realized he had no chance against Steven, began to whine. " 'Smy gun. 'Smine. Gimme."

The uniform man reached them, nodded briefly. Steven released the gun with a shrug. The boy skipped away into the crowd. As he went, he dropped another throwdown. Steven decided it did not sound like a shot at all, yet at the time—

He turned to the man in front of him, middle-aged, competent yet oddly defensive. "Collins, isn't it?" he asked.

"Yes, Sergeant. Harvey Collins. Tommy's Dr White's son. He's all right."

"I wasn't worrying about the boy. I was thinking about that gun. Did you see it? If it's genuine, could be valuable."

Collins shook his head. "Won't be. Guarantee that. Father's a collector. Keeps the real thing under lock and key. A copy most like."

"Looked genuine enough to me."

"Maybe—but White says a lot of imitations came out of Italy when this collecting craze started. Gunsmiths were turning out wheellocks, flintlocks, what-have-you, hoping to cash in." He looked quizzically at Steven. "Interesting collection, Sergeant. Take you round sometime, if you like."

"Yes. Should be worth looking at." The two men moved over to the edge of the footpath, stood gazing out over the mass of cars. "Something wrong with the kid, isn't there?" Steven asked.

Collins had apparently been waiting for his comment. "Yes. Congenital brain damage, I think. Interfered with the growth pattern, physically and mentally. Been here six years, myself, and young Tommy—well, he's been like that, exactly like that, ever since I first came across him."

Steven knew what he meant by "exactly like that". The stunted growth, fragile bone formation, white strengthless hands, vacant eyes.

"Six years! How old d'you reckon he is?"

Collins shrugged. "Eighteen. Twenty. Must be."

"And his parents?"

"The Whites? He's Dean of Science at the tech. She paints. Both sound people. Pity really—their only son."

Steven was silent. Other people's lives, he thought. Collins cleared his throat.

"Mind if I ask you something?"

"Not at all. Fire ahead."

10

"We ask for reinforcements. And one turns out to be a detective."

"Ours not to reason why," said Steven lightly.

"No. I suppose not," Collins smiled knowingly. "One of Jonas Peacock's hunches, eh? Work with him, don't you? Uncle or something."

Steven sighed. "Inspector Peacock happens to be my wife's uncle," he said evenly. "And I met Kylie through my association with him, not vice versa."

Collins grinned. "Rib you about it, do they? Think you've got it made. That's all they know." His mouth twisted slightly. "Old Jonas would be twice as tough. Tiger for protocol—discipline. I should know. Did my training with him."

Steven looked at Collins with renewed interest, was about to speak, when he noticed the traffic flow was beginning to lessen.

He looked back. At the next intersection, an officer was directing traffic into side streets, away from the centre of the town. As the street cleared, people began spilling on to the roadway, anxious not to miss any of the action.

Uniform police deftly shepherded them back to the footpath. "Back, please. Leave room for the horses. Back, please."

Only a few minutes were needed to clear two blocks, leaving the road wide and empty, a vast stage for an exciting play. The audience stood on the footpath expectant, waiting.

"Going in for the contest?" Steven asked Collins. "Y'know, pick the outlaws."

Collins shook his head. "Local personnel not eligible. One of our fellows—" he paused, called softly. "Hey, Lance!"

A traffic officer standing a short distance from them turned, moved closer. "Everything right on schedule," he laughed. "Bring on the baddies."

Collins introduced Steven. "Lance Brendon, Transport. Steven Arrow, Detective-Sergeant."

Brendon's eyebrows climbed a little, his lean handsome face twisted into a surprised grimace, but before he could ask, Why a detective? Collins interposed.

"We're talking about the bandits, Lance." He turned to Steven.

11

"Lance here rooms with Joe Blaney. Constable Joe Blaney. One of the outlaws. What's he wearing, Lance?"

The officer pulled a comic face.

"You've got me there. They're keeping that very hush-hush. But I do know something you don't." He leaned towards Steven, whispered, "I'm driving the getaway car."

"Getaway car! I thought this was a horse show!"

Lance grinned amiably. "It is, too. But no one will see the car. Behind the pub, The Golden Horseshoe. Y'see, the baddies rob the bank, have a running fight with the sheriff, retreat to the saloon. Joe ducks right through, leaves them to it while I rush him back home."

He nudged Steven with a conspiratorial leer. "Way we figured, Joe'll be back on the beat—in uniform—before the show's over. Not bad, eh?"

"Not bad," agreed Steven. "Put quite a few people off the scent."

A slight frown puckered the traffic officer's forehead. "Hope they're on time. I'm supposed to be on point at two."

Steven looked towards the eastern end of the street. A large dray was being moved into the next street where several white-painted drums had been set up at intervals.

"Looks like things are moving right now," he said.

"Goodoh!" cried Lance. "See you!"

As he darted off towards the hotel, the outlaws rode into view, four abreast, big men, faintly tinged with menace. Good riders, they sat their horses easily, carelessly. A clue, thought Steven. Could be members of the riding school which had lent gear to Barne Evans to decorate his shop window.

Three of the men were dressed in plaid shirts, bright bandannas, chaps, ten-gallon hats. The fourth was a gambler, white ruffled shirt, gaudy weskit, tight black pants and jacket, black hat.

All were extremely hirsute, heavy false eyebrows and villainous moustaches covering their faces as effectively as masks.

They entered the main street, entirely oblivious of the spectators, as though they were indeed riding into the dusty street of a deserted cowtown.

12

Not speaking, hardly looking to right or left, they stopped at the hitching rail erected a few yards from the bank, dismounted, tied their horses with practised ease.

Casually they sauntered towards the bank, paused, made a swift scrutiny of the "empty" street. The gambler entered the building, followed quickly by two of the cowboys. The remaining outlaw draped himself against the wall, hand on gun, alert, dangerous.

There was a murmur of amusement from the crowd as the sheriff and his deputy swaggered round the corner. They walked slowly, weighted down by artillery tied to their legs in approved killer style.

The cowboy on guard was instantly wary. He pulled his gun from its holster, stood ready, gun hidden by his body.

From inside the bank came one high-pitched scream then silence. The sheriff swung towards the sound, guns appearing in his hands. He pranced forward but the cowboy watcher shot first.

The sheriff dived for the dray, his deputy close behind.

They shot at the outlaw. The outlaw shot back, crouched behind a handy water trough.

The other three emerged from the bank, carrying bars of "gold", canvas bags ostentatiously marked with dollar signs. They joined in the shooting but the sheriff's accurate gunfire kept them away from their horses.

The outlaws fell back, shooting all the time, taking advantage of every bit of cover. The brave sheriff and his deputy followed, dodging from oil drum to water trough, from water trough to oil drum.

The outlaws retreated past the spot where Steven and Collins were standing, dived for the shelter of The Golden Horseshoe.

The "saloon" was a simple building with a wooden balcony running around the second storey. Presently one of the outlaws appeared on this balcony, shouting defiance.

Shots were exchanged, the sheriff was wounded, the outlaw died dramatically and entertainingly over the rail of the balcony.

Immediately someone emerged to drag the "body" inside the building even as the sheriff rushed the saloon, both guns blazing.

13

In the sudden quiet, Steven heard the sharp click of horse's hooves. He turned to see a horse being led by a nineteenth-century clerk, resplendent in high collar and heavy watch chain.

The doors of the saloon opened. Two of the outlaws came out with hands held high. The third was unceremoniously dragged to where the horse was patiently waiting, heaved over the saddle.

The sheriff lofted his hat to the crowd in acknowledgement of the cheers as the triumphant procession wandered back along the street, the sheriff urging the captives ahead with elaborate gun flourishes, the deputy leading the horse with its limp burden.

Steven wondered how many people realized that the bandit dressed as a gambler was still missing, and if Blaney had successfully carried out his intention of being on the beat again before the end of the stylized western drama.

Collins shifted his position, grinned at Steven. "Pretty good, eh? Went off very well."

Steven nodded. "Right on the dot. And everyone seems to have enjoyed it."

"Yeh. Well, I guess we'd better open up the streets again. Back to work, eh?"

Steven sent a speculative glance towards the east. The little company had less than half a block to go. The dray had already disappeared, most of the oil drums. There remained only the crowd which had spilled across the roadway to see the show.

Uniform men were urging them back to the footpath, a pleasant task as everyone was laughing, discussing the robbery.

As soon as the way was clear, the closed intersections were reopened and cars were rolling bumper to bumper again.

Steven worked his way along the street towards the police station. He kept to the edge of the crowd intensely aware that Collins was following close behind.

He was wondering why the local man seemed to be so interested in him when he saw Tommy White again. He heard him first, the slurred voice saying, "Bang, you're dead". There were no accompanying detonations so Steven concluded he had run out of throwdowns.

Bending down to pick up a parcel dropped by an elderly woman, he saw Tommy out of the corner of his eye.

14

He stiffened, checked his first amazed discovery as he handed over the parcel, looked back at Collins. Quickly he signalled "danger", began to walk towards Tommy.

The crowd did not see Tommy as a danger. They exclaimed over his costume, the silver buckles, the high cowboy boots and yes, the gun.

By the time Steven reached Tommy, Collins was beside him. "Good grief! A Luger! Where'd he get hold of that?"

"Don't know. But we'll find out." Steven turned to the cowboy, said genially. "Hello, Tommy. Killed any baddies lately?"

Tommy swung to face him, lifted the gun, mouthed his usual greeting, "Bang, you're dead".

"I'm dead," agreed Steven, gently propelling the boy through the crowd into the comparative lull of a side street.

"Play dead then. Like he did. Fell down proper. Off the stairs. Kerrumph!"

"Who fell down, Tommy?"

"He did. The bad man. The black bandit. Baddie. Baddie. I killed him dead. Bang. Bang. Bang."

His attention wandered to a cluster of children at the end of the short street. "Gig ride. Wanna gig ride," he cried, jumping up and down, excited by the prospect.

Steven snarled mentally at his luck in picking the street where gig rides were being provided for the children.

He held Tommy firmly. "Tommy, tell me about the man."

Tommy squirmed. "Wanna gig ride. Gig ride. Wanna gig ride."

"Tell me about the man first. The man who fell down."

Tommy paused momentarily. A skinny finger jabbed at Steven's chest. "No star. No star. Got no star," he chanted.

He started fighting the firm hold again. "Wanna gig ride. Wanna gig ride." He wriggled energetically, his voice going higher, higher, frightened.

Steven looked apprehensively at the people passing the top of the street. Someone was bound to notice soon.

"Right you are, fella. We'll get you a gig ride. Here!" He lifted the slight figure to his shoulder, turned to Collins. "Get the marshal, will you? The sheriff fella."

15

He carried Tommy over to the gig now halted opposite the police station. There was something familiar about the girl holding the reins and he breathed a sigh of relief when she turned her head enough for him to recognize her.

"Kathy! Do me a favour. Make room for this one."

The girl hesitated. "They're supposed to stand in line. Oh, all right. If it's important."

Steven lifted Tommy into the gig. "There you are, fella. All set. Here, I'll mind your gun." Deftly he palmed the gun, stepped back on to the footpath.

He was examining the weapon when he was joined by Collins and the sheriff, a man named Jeff Cottar.

"What's up?" he asked. "Harvey said there's trouble."

Steven shrugged. "We think. Maybe we're wrong. Hope so. See this Luger? Empty. But fired recently. Tommy White had it. Says he shot a baddie. On some stairs. But he won't talk to me. No star, he says. So you're it. Play up the cowboy bit, will you?"

The gig ride finished. Tommy came racing over to claim his gun. Steven handed it to him reluctantly, looked at Cottar.

The sheriff leaned over the boy. "Hi, there, pardner. Hear tell you got rid of a rustler for me. Where'd he be?"

Tommy looked up at him, big-eyed.

"Going to claim the bounty, pardner?" persisted the sheriff. "Might be a few hundred dollars out on that varmint."

Tommy hiccupped. "Bounty. A bounty. Me?"

"Could be, cowboy. But I gotta see him first. Might be one of them thar varmints been rustling all them cattle lately."

Cottar, in his rôle of sheriff, had captured Tommy completely. He nodded vigorously, scampered along the street past the police station. At the south gate to the recreation grounds, he paused, looked back.

Satisfied that Cottar was following, he hurried on to the corner, turned into Kensington Avenue, passed the Petone Technical Institute, turned the corner, stopped at the second house on the left.

Steven looked at the house. Long, low, with old-fashioned bow windows. Curtains drawn. Windows shut. No one at home. Down town, probably, like everyone else.

16

"Looks like a false alarm," said Cottar with relief. "Tommy said stairs. No stairs in that house."

"Oh, there are stairs all right," said Steven quietly, pointing towards the garage at the back of the section. "Must be. That's a flat above the garage. Stairs will lead to that."

They walked down the driveway, watching the house for signs of movement. But no one was home. No one was interested.

From the corner of the house they saw the stairs leading to the flat above the garage—and the body lying spreadeagled in the shadow of the lower steps.

Steven moved forward with Collins, mentally checking the appearance of the body, the old-time clothes, black suit, bright weskit, white ruffled shirt now stained with red.

A tired wind stirred other parts of the scattered disguise, black stetson, false moustache, false eyebrows.

"It's Joe Blaney," breathed Collins.

"Yes. Joe Blaney," agreed Steven. "About an hour ago, I'd say. Must be."

That would fit. Blaney had rushed home to change, had never reached the flat. When? Five minutes to two? Two o'clock? Yes, an hour ago, at least.

Steven stepped two paces to the right, looked down the drive. Tommy was standing by the gate, absorbed in the mechanism of his gun. Jeff Cottar was bending over him, talking in a quick urgent manner, Tommy taking little or no notice.

Steven felt Collins move over to join him, heard the local man's swift intake of breath. "Good God! You don't think—— you can't mean—Tommy——?"

"Why not?" said Steven softly. "He had the gun."

17

CHAPTER II

THE GREY POLICE car paused briefly at the pavement, disgorged its single passenger, swung round, sped away again.

Detective-Inspector Jonas Peacock nodded at the uniformed man guarding the gate but made no move to enter. He stood on the edge of the footpath examining the house, the quiet street. By the time Steven reached the gateway, he was facing the roadway scrutinizing the closed windows of the house opposite.

"Afternoon, sir. Thought I heard a car."

Peacock grunted. "Anyone home over there?" he asked, waving his hand towards the other side of the street.

"Not a soul. We've made the rounds."

Peacock nodded. "That gate lead to the rec., does it?" he asked, pointing to the wrought-iron gate let into the brick wall at the blind end of the street. "Always left open like that?"

"Mostly. Except on match days maybe. Nobody on the rec. either. Everyone seems to be up town."

"Yes. Otherwise we'd be swamped by the vultures."

Steven smiled. Peacock must have been surprised to find none of the dear public gawping at the visual evidence of police interest. Two police cars parked behind a green Standard of near vintage age, police personnel coming and going.

"Get anything out of the boy?"

"No. Both Jeff Cottar and I had a go but—" He shrugged. "Difficult subject."

"Jeff Cottar is what exactly?"

"President of the Business Men's Club. Organizer and what-have-you of Ponderosa Day."

"He's the sheriff fellow you told me about?"

"Yes, sir."

18

Peacock nodded, still made no move to enter the guarded gate. His fingers fished into a waistcoat pocket, brought out the inevitable packet of gum. Deftly he extracted a pellet, placed it in his mouth, closed the wrapping around the remainder of the packet, replaced it in his pocket.

"Short street. Quiet. Fellow come through the rec., even down Kensington Avenue—hardly be noticed."

It was hardly a street, merely an opening created to accommodate the eastern gate of the recreation grounds. A corner house with one other behind, both sides. Hardly a street.

Peacock turned, stared thoughtfully at the massive building immediately behind the two houses on the south side.

"The old tech., eh? Years since I've been down this way. Used to be houses right down. Now they've built themselves a new block, I see. Flash. The old building looks kind of small. Windows on the rec. still, I suppose?"

"Yes, sir. We have a man there, checking to see if anyone was seen on the rec. around two."

Peacock glanced at him. "But you don't like your chances, eh? Everyone got his head down. Still, may be the odd one."

Steven cleared his throat. "It's called the Petone Technical Institute now, sir. Cover the whole block eventually. They own or are negotiating to own these two houses here and six or seven on the south side."

Peacock looked slightly startled, nodded briefly. "Of course. Of course. Whittaker here yet?"

"Yes, sir. Dr Whittaker is waiting."

At last Peacock ambled towards the gate. "Located the people who live here yet?"

"Not yet. Gregg's simple enough. Bank clerk. But Mrs Gregg—she'd be in the crowd somewhere."

"Hmm," said Peacock, began to walk slowly along the drive, Steven following at a discreet distance.

They reached the corner of the house. Peacock paused, looked back at the gateway, then towards the stair leading to the garage flat. He nodded to himself, strode briskly forwards.

"Hello, Bob," he greeted the man in the lounge suit. "Thanks for waiting."

19

Whittaker eyed him dourly. "Thought I might as well. Knew you wouldn't be too long."

Peacock squatted beside the body, momentarily lifting the covering blanket. "Didn't know what hit him, did he?" he said, straightening. "Instant, would you say?"

"I'd say. Very instant. Straight through the heart."

"Lucky shot?"

"Careful one more likely."

Peacock turned to Steven. "Worked out where he was when he was hit?"

"On the stairs. About the third step. Blood on the sixth step. He fell forwards then rolled off. And there's this."

He indicated a fresh white scar on the surface of the green-painted concrete wall.

"And the boy?"

"Waiting here, we think. Behind the hydrangea. Those would be his flowers."

Steven pointed to the hydrangea, heavy with new spring growth, screening the west end of the patio. On the dark earth beneath lay a scattered offering of child-plucked marigolds.

"Found any bullets yet?"

"One only. Damaged some but enough. Nine mille."

"Notified forensic."

"Yes, sir. On the way."

Peacock nodded, looked around, questing. "Where's the boy?"

"We took him home. At least, Collins did."

"Oh," Peacock frowned. "Why?"

Steven faced him squarely. "He was getting upset, sir. We—Jeff Cottar and I—we made the mistake of trying to question him like an ordinary person. Collins stopped us. Said we could do some damage. Better leave it to someone who knew how to get through."

"Collins said that, did he?" Peacock softly. "Constable Harvey Collins?"

"Yes, sir," said Steven doggedly. That emphasis on Collins' rank, or lack of it, was not unintentional.

"And this Jeff Cottar? Where is he?"

"Gone back up town, sir. He's running this Ponderosa Day.

20

Scheduled to introduce some radio people putting on a show."

Peacock stared at Steven, deepset eyes flint-like, expressionless. Finally, he shrugged, turned to Whittaker.

"What d'you think, Bob? About the White boy?"

Whittaker smiled frostily. " 'Fraid I agree with the sergeant, old man. Needs expert handling."

"D'you think he could've fired the shot?"

"Of course. Providing only one bullet in the gun."

"What d'you mean?"

"A full magazine. He'd have shot the lot. Cowboys and Indians, y'know."

Peacock digested this observation on cowboy behaviour, turned to Steven. "Only one bullet, you said."

"So far. We'll be doing a square search but——We don't really expect to find any more. If he'd missed that first shot, Blaney would've dived for cover."

"There'll be only one bullet," said Whittaker drily.

"Pretty confident, you think. Came here to shoot a man down with only one bullet?"

"I didn't say that. Could've had a full magazine—unloaded afterwards."

"Tommy White?"

"I wasn't thinking about Tommy White," snapped Whittaker. "Now, if you don't need me, I have more important things to do."

He stamped off down the drive in a high temper. Peacock stared after him. "What's eating him?"

"The Whites are friends of his, I believe, sir. Thought we were nuts even to think Tommy had anything to do with it."

The upraised eyebrows settled down into their accustomed place as the inspector moved over to the garage stairs.

They were constructed in stark simplicity, little more than a ladder set against the wall, the barest concession to safety being a light metal railing held by three widely-spaced uprights.

He stood on the third step, then mounted to the fourth to make allowances for Blaney's extra height. The white scar of the ricochet conveniently behind him, he studied the small yard.

Steven moved to be in line with the stairs, the hydrangea.

"No," said Peacock sharply. "You'd need to be over nine feet tall to get me through the treads. Try the patio. Hmph. A bit higher. What about that table there?"

Steven climbed carefully on to the small wrought-iron table, found to his surprise he was level with Peacock even though hunched down to Tommy's height.

Peacock grunted, signalled his satisfaction.

"Have to be facing you, of course. Trajectory horizontal with slight uplift. Yes, that would do it. Bit obvious though."

Steven dropped lightly to the ground, deftly catching the edge of the table as it tipped sideways.

Peacock came down the few steps, spent some time stepping out distances then paused again by the stair looking up at the flat.

"One thing we know. He wasn't shot from the flat. But we'll have to have a look at it. Got a key?"

Before Steven could answer, they were startled by the sound of a shouted command, the scream of rubber.

"What the——" he cried, running towards the drive. Steven joined him, looking towards the gate.

A transport-department car straddled the footpath with the uniform man talking to the driver. As they watched, the black car swooshed out into the road again, curved back to park against the kerb out of sight.

"Brendon," said Steven unnecessarily.

The traffic officer came down the drive at an easy lope, white shirt gleaming, jacket slung carelessly over his right shoulder.

"Where is he?" he demanded as he drew level.

Steven and Peacock moved aside, indicating the covered figure under the stairs.

Brendon walked slowly over, stood there. He made no attempt to remove the blanket, simply stood there in silence. His hand lifted once to remove his cap.

Peacock opened his mouth to speak, stopped. At last, Brendon turned towards them. "They told me over the blower. Said I had to turn the car in for something."

"Routine," said Peacock briskly. "You've worked with police enough to know the way we do things."

22

Brendon shrugged. "Looking for bloodstains and stuff, are you? Could be some. Joe had a bleeding nose Wednesday night. Brought him home in the car."

He spoke listlessly, uninterested in their reaction to this disclosure. Peacock looked at Steven, grimaced.

"We don't think he was shot in the car, officer," he said.

Brendon shook his head. "That's what I can't get, Inspector. Why would they shoot Joe? Anyone? Shoot him?"

"Could've been an accident. The gun—the one we think was used—was in the possession of Tommy White. Know him?"

"Yes. I know him. Everyone does. Did he——?"

"Perhaps. Unfortunately, Tommy isn't exactly an ideal witness. Anyway, if he is responsible, it would be an accident. Manslaughter. He's hardly capable of planning a murder."

"But you think he did the actual shooting?" Brendon's eyes narrowed dangerously.

Peacock paused, considering. "That's the way it looks. At the moment. But we're going to be careful about this one. We don't like police personnel being killed. So we'll be asking questions, tough questions of anyone and everyone, till we prove to our own satisfaction it was an accident."

"Anything I can do to help," said Brendon, the formula reply sounding flat and distant.

Steven wondered how often he had heard those words, how little they generally meant. He looked down the drive at the sound of another car. Men were climbing out, men with cameras, other equipment.

"The boffins are here," he said.

"Right," said Peacock. "We'll go up to the flat. Got a key?" He turned to the transport officer.

"Yes," said Brendon. "I've got a key."

He led the way up the stairs, hand searching his pockets. Peacock followed with Steven close behind. Brendon opened the door, stood back on the small slotted platform to allow them to enter ahead of him.

Steven paused only to look down on the two men with cameras coming around the corner of the house. They glanced up incuriously, moved over to the base of the stairs.

23

The flat was merely a large partitioned room, the same area as the garage and extensive workshop beneath. It could have been dull and dreary, but someone had used imagination and foresight.

An island containing electric range and bench line refrigerator divided the main room into open-plan kitchen and lounge furnished with old but comfortable pieces, bright rugs on the cork tiled floor.

"All mod. cons, eh?" said Peacock. "What d'you do for a bath?"

"We go down to the house," said Brendon shortly.

"And what if the Greggs are out?"

Brendon shrugged. "They leave a back door key in the wash-house. That door's never locked."

Peacock looked at Steven who nodded. "Wash-house door was open. I thought it was the back door but it's quite separate. Sort of porch. Washing machine. Dryer. Handbasin, and a toilet off."

Peacock walked over to the window, looked down at the back of the house. "Door's shut now. That the way you found it?"

"No, sir. It was slightly ajar. That's why I checked. The back door's locked. The actual back door, that is."

Peacock turned to Brendon. "And the key? Where's it kept?"

"In the loo. There's a hook in the lid of the cistern."

Steven shook his head. "Not there. The cistern lid's been lifted, leaning against the wall. I noticed that hook. Wondered what it was for."

"Hmph," said Peacock. "Who else knew about the key?"

Brendon shrugged. "Not many. Joe. Me. The Greggs."

"You mention it to anyone?"

"Possibly. Don't remember anyone in particular though."

"But it was a joke, wasn't it?" sneered Peacock. "Keeping the house key in the loo! Sort of thing you'd giggle over in the pub."

Brendon stiffened, obviously angry, but he said nothing. Peacock's mouth turned down with displeasure as he faced Steven.

"All right. Get them to dust the wash-house."

Steven hurried to convey Peacock's message to the men work-

24

ing below. It took only a few minutes to arrange but when he returned Peacock was already seated opposite Brendon, questioning him.

Brendon sat forward, jacket carefully folded on the back of the chair. "The last time I saw Joe was when I let him off here. I stopped long enough for him to get out, that's all. Running a bit late." He sighed. "If I'd waited around maybe I'd have heard the shot, maybe seen something."

"Or even prevented it. If you'd brought Blaney right in, you'd still be backing out as he was dashing up the stairs. Maybe it wouldn't have happened." He paused but the transport man gazed back stonily. "You didn't see anything at all? Hear anything?"

"Nothing. Of course, I wasn't expecting anything, was I? I knew the Greggs were up town. Everyone in the street. Everyone."

"Except Joe Blaney, you, and Tommy White."

Brendon stared at Peacock as though trying to read something into his remark but the bland face betrayed nothing.

"Tommy White! Yes, he must've been here but I didn't see him, Inspector. He wasn't in sight. Must've been hiding."

"Must've been. Tell me, how many people knew Blaney was one of the bandits?"

"Most of us, I guess. We all thought it a bit zaney. Y'know, a policeman playing outlaw. Something to do with the security bit, I believe. Sergeant Fairbrother insisted on one of the bandits being police and Joe was it."

"When you say 'most of us'—who exactly? Police? Transport? The general public?"

"No, not the general public. Though Cottar knew, of course. Possibly one or two of the committee."

"Cottar's the one who dreamed up Ponderosa Day?"

"Yes. President of the Business Men's Club. Secretary of the Ratepayers. You name it, he's done it. Arranged the whole thing, I believe. Played the sheriff. You must've seen him!"

"Not yet! Haven't been up town so far. The other three bandits would know?"

"Well, yes, of course. Had to. Had a couple of practices

25

together. Timing, y'know. But what difference does that make?"

"At this stage, we don't know. We're still gathering information. Right now it looks like an accidental shooting but it might not be. There could be someone who thinks he has a valid reason for killing Blaney."

He paused, watching the other man carefully. "What's your guess, Brendon? You were closer to Blaney than anyone. Why was Blaney killed? Because Tommy White really believed Blaney was a big bad bandit? Or is there another reason, a better reason?"

He waited quietly but no answer came.

"What about—because he was Joe Blaney? Anyone hate him enough to go that far?" His lips thinned as the traffic man wearily shook his head. "All right. What about—because he was a policeman?"

Brendon's jaw tightened, his eyes flickered momentarily towards the closed bedroom door, returned to fasten themselves once again on Peacock's face.

"That means you're going to search the flat. That right?"

"Yes, it means we're going to search the flat," agreed Peacock mildly. "Worry you at all?"

"No. Not at all," replied Brendon confidently.

CHAPTER III

THE SLOWLY-BUILDING tension was broken by a knock on the door. Steven hurriedly came back to life, opened the door.

Constable Harvey Collins entered, spoke to Peacock. "The Greggs are here, sir. Waiting in the house with Constable Taylor."

"Good! Any trouble locating either of them?"

"No, sir. Gregg was at the bank. Mrs Gregg was watching the quick-draw contest."

Peacock nodded. "You took Tommy White home, didn't you? How did you explain things to his mother?"

"The barest facts, sir. A man had been shot. Tommy had the gun. Advised her to keep Tommy indoors till you came."

Peacock climbed unhurriedly to his feet. "Well, the next step. Search this flat. You'll help, Collins. Take this room. We'll do the bedroom."

The narrow bedroom was utilitarian. Two beds, set lengthwise, one to the right against the outer wall, the other to the left against the partition. Curtained wardrobe space at each end of the room, two wall mirrors and, by each bed, a lowboy, one conspicuously empty, the other cluttered with living: clock, photograph, library books with notebook atop.

Neatly set out on the bed beneath the long dormer window was a summer uniform, white helmet sitting squarely on the pillow.

Peacock walked over to the bed, picked up each item, retaining only the day-book after glancing briefly at its first page.

"All right, Sergeant. You take that end."

Brendon moved across the room, looked out of the window, turned to watch them, jacket folded over his left arm.

27

Steven pulled aside the masking curtain of the wardrobe, began to search the few items of clothing hanging there, comfortable clothing of the tweedy type—Blaney's from the letters, bills in the pockets, the photograph album lying on the shoe shelf.

Collins came to the door, a sheaf of papers in his hand. Peacock took them, riffled through, placed them with the articles accumulating on the bed.

Steven worked his way down the lowboy at the head of Blaney's bed. Nothing interesting, only neatly folded clothing and, in the corner of one of the drawers, a packet of letters, the return address—Chief-Inspector C. J. Blaney, CID Auckland.

Thoughtfully he stood up, gazing absently at the items on the top. There was something wrong, changed since he came into the room.

He fingered the two library books, both covering sailing voyages around the world, moved the ballpoint, studied the studio portrait of an attractive girl. He looked at Brendon, indicating the photograph.

"Joe's girl. Arline Muir," said Brendon curtly.

Steven nodded, glanced at Peacock, found the senior man watching him. He knows something, thought Steven, he's wondering if I'm awake.

He turned back to the lowboy. There had been something. He was sure. The photograph. The books. The ballpoint. Of course, the ballpoint! There had been a notebook also, a black notebook, thick but pocket size.

"Where'd the notebook go?" Steven asked casually. "The one on the lowboy?"

Peacock grinned wryly. "All right, Brendon. It was a good try. Hand it over."

Brendon seemed about to deny the allegation, hesitated, shrugged, produced the notebook from the folds of his jacket. He handed it to Peacock, turned on his heel, left the room.

Peacock opened the notebook, quickly scanned the first few pages, grimaced sourly, placed it in his side pocket.

"All right, Collins," he said, indicating the heap on the bed. "Put those in the car."

Steven followed the inspector out of the bedroom, through the main room, on to the stairs. Preparations were being made to remove Blaney's body. Steven looked for Brendon, saw a glimmer of white shirt in the shadow of the open wash-house door.

The transport man stayed there, almost out of sight, until the stretcher-bearers disappeared down the drive, then he came out, stood in the full sun, watched them descend.

He waited till the inspector was almost abreast, said briskly, "Permission to go, sir. I have to report back."

Peacock nodded. "Yes, you may go," he said indifferently.

"I'll need the car, sir," Brendon suggested tentatively.

Peacock stiffened. "What were your exact instructions, Brendon?" he asked roughly.

"Report here and turn in my car, sir."

"Well, you've turned in your car. We can't release it to you again now. You'll have to make it under your own steam."

"Sir!" began Brendon then stopped.

"Well? Haven't you got a car of your own?"

"Yes, sir. The Standard out front. But I'll probably have to bring back a motorbike."

"Oh, well in that case." Peacock spoke to a uniform man standing at the corner of the house. "See this man gets back to Hutt Road," he instructed.

He turned away, no longer interested, examined the patio, the back of the house. He paused on the step of the small room housing the wash-house, glanced swiftly around, moved over to the toilet door, opened it, stared thoughtfully at the open cistern lid, the empty hook welded on to its inner surface.

"Tommy White have the key?" he asked abruptly.

"Couldn't say, sir," said Steven. "We didn't search him."

"No, of course not. It might have upset him, eh?" He recrossed the room to open the back door, waited till Steven had entered the airy kitchen, closed the door noisily.

"The back door was locked, you say."

"It was locked—then," agreed Steven.

Peacock stood inside the doorway, eyes alert, while his fingers were busy with the inevitable packet of juicyfruit. Footsteps

29

sounded from the front of the house, a young fresh-faced constable appeared at the inner doorway.

"Good afternoon, sir," he said carefully. "Mr and Mrs Gregg are waiting in the front room."

"Taylor, isn't it?"

"Yes, sir."

Peacock nodded, dropped his voice. "How much do they know?"

"That Joe Blaney was shot. That's all, Inspector."

"Have they been talking together at all?"

"No, sir. Missus is at the window, watching. Mister is prowling round like a caged bear."

He stepped aside, allowing them to look through the dining-room, through the open glass doors, into the front-room. His description of Basil Gregg fell neatly into place when Steven saw the hunched shoulders, the shambling walk, the shock of grey hair.

Mrs Gregg seemed tiny by comparison, pale face, pale hair, soft blue dress. She sat in the windowseat watching the activity outside. She did not seem alarmed by what had happened, only decently sad, decorously interested.

She turned as they entered the room, acknowledged introductions with a slight lift of her hand. Gregg stopped his restless pacing, stared at them resentfully, flopped into a large armchair.

"I won't keep you long," said Peacock. "Just want you to tell me anything you know about this."

Mrs Gregg smiled gently. "Less than nothing, I'm afraid. Only what Constable Collins told us."

"That your tenant Joe Blaney had been shot?"

Mrs Gregg winced delicately, looked at her hands. "I'm not stupid, Inspector. I know it was not an accident."

"Oh, do you? Not usual for people to go around taking pot shots at others, is it?"

"No, but he was a policeman. I was always afraid something might happen. Something like this."

Her husband snorted. "Fiddle!" he declared. "Nobody's safer than a policeman. Nobody!"

Mrs Gregg's lips compressed ever so slightly. "Not this time, dear. Not this time. And you know I've always said——"

Gregg interrupted. "The inspector is not in the least bit interested in your premonitions, Marion. He simply wants to know what we were doing at time of death. Correct, Inspector?"

Peacock nodded. "Quite correct, Mr Gregg."

"Well, I've been at work all day. Some of us are working, y'know, for all the hooha going on up town."

"I gather it wasn't your bank that was robbed?"

"You can bet on that. Got more common. Asking for trouble, they were. Lending their premises for a silly stunt like that."

"I understand only the entrance was used," said Peacock gently. "And stringent security measures were taken."

Gregg snorted again. "Lucky nothing went wrong. Could've, y'know. Then you'd look a bit sick, wouldn't you. As it was——" he paused, looked towards the window, frowning.

"Well, your colleagues at the bank will confirm, no doubt."

He turned to the woman. "Now, what about you, Mrs Gregg?"

"But, Inspector, you don't honestly believe——"

"Don't be a nit, Marion. The inspector has to ask these questions. He has to ask everyone where they were. It's part of the job."

"Oh! Well, I've been up town most of the day, Inspector. Since eleven or thereabouts."

"Alone?"

"No. With my sister. We lunched up town, early. Then had a wander around looking at the exhibits."

"You saw the bank robbery?"

"Oh, yes. Couldn't miss that." A faint pink touched her pale cheeks and Steven wondered which particular recollection caused it.

"Did you know Constable Blaney was to be one of the bandits?"

Mrs Gregg started. "No. Was he?" She frowned. "Goodness! Joe! Which one would he be? No, even now I can't pick him."

"Mr Gregg?"

The shaggy man shook his head. "No. Never mentioned it to me. Funny thing for a policeman to do, wasn't it?"

31

"Part of the security measures, Mr Gregg. Less chance of infiltration."

Gregg's untrimmed eyebrows jounced. "I see. Good idea. Sorry! Thought the whole scheme completely wild, childish. Now I realize you weren't so off hand, after all."

"We don't exactly advertise, Mr Gregg."

"No, that's only too obvious. And you don't tell us much either."

The angry light was back in his eyes. "Don't you think it's about time you put us in the picture, Inspector? I understood Joe was shot here. Now, it sounds as though it might've been up town."

Peacock considered. "No. I'll admit that's a possibility we have to look into. Eliminate. But we don't seriously contend it happened that way. Too many things would have to be planted. The bullet, for instance. The gun."

"Ah! You've got the gun then. A rifle?"

"Why a rifle, Mr Gregg?"

"Well," Gregg looked surprised. "It could only be a rifle surely, a rifle or some such. Hand guns are illegal."

"Not for everyone. You have hand guns at the bank, don't you?"

"Yes. Smith and Wesson's mostly. One Luger. Only selected personnel have access."

"D'you have access, Mr Gregg?"

"Sometimes. When necessary."

"So you'd have access to the Luger?"

"The Luger? It was a Luger then?"

"It was a Luger," Peacock agreed mildly. "Wonder if it could be the same one."

"Basil!" cried Mrs Gregg. "Basil! You didn't——"

Gregg swung round on his wife. "Don't be daft, Marion. I've been at work all afternoon. About six people can vouch for me."

"So you knew it happened this afternoon?" Peacock's voice was deliberately soft.

"Why, yes, didn't it?" His eyes narrowed, his lip curled cynically. "That wasn't a slip, Inspector. I had a perfectly legitimate reason for knowing. After all, you did say Joe was

32

one of the bandits. So it had to be ths afternoon. Besides I saw him myself around lunchtime."

"You saw him? Where?"

"With Lance—Lance Brendon. In the patrol car. Ordinary clothes. I wondered. Because I thought Joe was on duty to-day."

"What d'you mean by ordinary clothes, Mr Gregg?"

"Well, dark suit coat anyway. Like I said. He was in the car. Only saw the top half of him."

"Would you say it was a black suit coat?"

"Yes, black. Soft white collar. Shoe string tie."

"A ruffled shirt?"

"A ruffled shirt," repeated Gregg slowly. "That's what was wrong. A ruffled shirt. Thought there was something odd. Decided it was the tie. Hadn't seen him in a shoestring before. But, of course, I must've seen the ruffled shirt."

"All right. You saw Blaney. In the patrol car. Which means you were outside the bank at the time."

"Well, yes. I take lunch hour from one to two. That's when I saw him." He paused, looked thoughtful. "That puts me out on the limb again, eh? Joe must've been killed before two."

"We think so."

Gregg shook his head, ran stubby fingers through his thick hair.

"So I don't have an alibi. Now, what did I do during my lunch break? I had a haircut. Patterson's near Cuba Street. Then I went for a walk. Down on the beach. Try to get down there every day if possible."

"Anyone see you?"

"Can't say for sure. No one on the beach anyway."

"You weren't interested in the pageant?"

"No. Thought it a lot of guff. Oh, I heard the shooting, of course. But I knew what it was all about."

"So you spent your time on the beach. Till about two?"

"That's right."

"Well, we'll check. Maybe someone did see you." He turned to Mrs Gregg. "How long has Blaney been staying here?"

Mrs Gregg frowned prettily. "Six months? Lance has been here over a year. Came when Jimmy had the flat, Jimmy

33

Torrens. Then Jimmy got married so Lance had to find some-one else to share."

"How did they get on together?"

"Very well. Joe's the amiable type. Fit in with anyone. Lance —well, of course, Lance—he's a bit temperamental. Y'know, blow his top over nothing then be right as rain in ten minutes. Always used to be rowing with Jimmy but he and Joe, I think Joe knew exactly how to handle him."

"So you'd say they've never had any serious disagreements?"

"Well, no, Inspector. I didn't say that at all. There was that business about Arline."

Mrs Gregg lifted her hands, spread them in front of her, examined them intently. She seemed oblivious of both the inspector's surprise and her husband's frantic gestures. When she raised her eyes, she looked directly at Gregg, spoke sweetly.

"He'll find out soon enough, dear. And it wasn't anything really. If we try to conceal—er—evidence it might blow up out of all proportion. Isn't that so, Inspector?"

Peacock choked slightly, nodded his head gravely. Gregg sighed, settled deeper into his chair.

Mrs Gregg smiled serenely. "Y'see, Inspector, Arline used to go with Lance. She was his girl."

"Arline Muir?"

"Yes. Oh, it was very serious. At least it seemed that way. Then all of a sudden she dropped Lance—dropped him just like that—and started going with Joe. Must've been a shock for Lance. He's the love 'em, leave 'em kind. This time he was the one who was left."

She giggled softly at the recollection. "Didn't like it at all. Poor Lance. Really went to town with Joe. But it all blew over. They were buddy-buddies again in no time. And Lance started going with Arline's flat mate, Judy Clark. Made a nice four-some."

"This was how long ago?" asked Peacock.

"July? No, August. The end of August."

Peacock nodded, veered off on another angle. "Was it gen-erally known you'd not be in to-day, Mrs Gregg?"

"But nobody stayed at home to-day, Inspector!"

34

She seemed surprised at his obtuseness. "Everybody went up town to-day. Everybody from around here anyway. Even old Mrs Davidson. And she hasn't been out of the house for years."

"She lives?"

"Opposite. Directly opposite. With her grand-daughter. I suppose you'll be talking to them, too."

"Yes. Routine. Everyone has to be interviewed. Now, one last question. Who opened the back door?"

"I did," said Gregg. "There's a spare key, Inspector. Kept on the key tidy in the kitchen. Y'see, we always lock the back door from the inside, go out the front."

"Of course," Peacock stood up. "Well, that's it. We'll have another look at the kitchen if you don't mind."

"Anything you want, Inspector."

"Thanks," said Peacock, pausing by the glass doors. "By the way, Mr Gregg, d'you always take your car to work?"

The innocent-sounding question caught Gregg off balance. He swung towards them, cheeks stained dark red, answered belligerently, "Of course not. Too damn close. Only take it when it's wet or when I have to go elsewhere. Like to-day. Had to go into Wellington first thing this morning. Bank business."

Peacock nodded, turned, walked through the intervening room, paused in the doorway of the kitchen, a narrow compact room occupying the whole width of the house except for the porch wash-house.

Large windows to the high stud ceiling overlooked the patio, the neatly-kept lawns and back garden.

Peacock went to the window over the sink, stared out at the stairway to the garage flat, examined the formica bench carefully, pointed out a slight scuffing of the surface. It could have been recent. It could have been an old marking.

He pulled a chair over, hopped lightly on to the bench, crouched to peer out of the fanlight. He nodded to himself, ran his finger along the edge of the open window, moved along the bench, checked the ledge of the next window.

"This window open when you came around?"

"Exactly the way it is now, sir. It's fixed as you see."

A half-inch steel bar screwed to the window frame and the

sill held the fanlight open a scant but permanent six inches. Peacock patted the window-ledge, jumped down from the bench, checked to see if he had left any marks, replaced the chair.

He turned to Steven. "Might be a good idea to have a talk with Tommy White now. The other side of the tech., isn't it?"

"Yes, sir. School house. Second from the main block."

The first signs of public interest were waiting at the gate, four school children avidly watching. Peacock ignored the audience, climbed aboard the police car, pulled out the black notebook as Steven shut the door.

"Before we go, you'd better have a look at this."

Steven took the book, stared in surprise at the first page.

"That's Collins' number, isn't it?"

"Yes, you're quite right. What was Brendon up to, d'you think? A bit obvious, wasn't he? Wanted us to notice. Or maybe he wanted Collins to notice."

Steven read the information on the first page, dates, detailed evidence, circumstantial but reasonably conclusive.

"Collins—" he began but Peacock shrugged.

"I don't know. I really don't know. There was an inquiry but I understood he was cleared. Not proven anyway. But now——"

He laughed bitterly. "Police never give up, do they? Especially when one of their own may be involved. Better look at the rest though. Collins isn't the only one for the chopper. They've all got their quota of probability."

Steven flipped through the book quickly. The first three pages were devoted to Collins, but every man on the local force seemed to have his number in that little black book, mostly one-page entries, some only one entry to the page. Other pages were covered with lists of dates, liberally ticked, lists of merchandise each marked with a date.

Steven could not guess the significance of the ticks but it was obvious Blaney had been investigating a series of burglaries committed at irregular intervals over the past two years, with Collins as the chief suspect.

CHAPTER IV

THE HOUSE ALLOTTED to the Whites was in cream-coloured roughcast, two storeyed, iron roofed, the northern face drowned in massed waves of ancient ivy.

Steven opened the low gate, expert eyes assessing the garden fringing the shaggy lawn. He decided the gardener was more enthusiastic than knowledgeable, despite the flaunting border of marigolds by the wire fence, and his impression was strengthened when they stepped on to the latticed porch.

Someone had spent time and labour scooping out pieces of pumice, planting them with succulents. Six separate containers, all neglected, plants crowding each other for space.

Steven swung round as the door opened and Alexander White stood framed in the doorway, brown hair lightly frosted, hazel eyes sharp, observant. He motioned them into the house, along a short passage, into an old fashioned kitchen-cum-living-room, a veritable farm kitchen, unexpected in a town dwelling.

A room of warmth and welcome. Too many chairs, an over-long table and, set in the far wall, a tremendous wood stove dwarfing that summer necessity, a small gas stove.

Steven could imagine students gathered here on wintry nights, work spread over the table, discussions going on till the last slab of wood in the huge stove settled into white ash.

White introduced his wife, thin to gauntness, tired blue eyes and nervous hands. He waved a vague invitation to seat themselves, selected a straight-backed chair by the window.

"You know why we are here," Peacock began.

White nodded. "Yes. A man has been shot. And Tommy had the gun which probably shot him."

"The man was Constable Joseph Blaney. The gun was a Luger.

37

Would you know anything about that, Dr White?"

The professor tilted his head, thought out his answer, spoke slowly. Steven was to find that this was characteristic when on unfamiliar ground. White never allowed himself to be bustled, never rushed into answers.

"I know about Lugers, Inspector. Of course! I know nothing about this particular one."

"But you are familiar with guns, hand guns?"

"I have a collection of hand guns, Inspector. No doubt you have already been told this. But not modern guns. Antiques."

"Would you say Tommy was familiar with guns?"

"With wheellocks, flintlocks, yes. Some of the earlier percussion instruments, yes. With modern guns?" He shrugged. "If you'd asked me that question this morning, Inspector, I'd have said he'd never handled a modern gun in his life."

"Would you think his being familiar with antiques would mean an easy transition to a Luger?"

White smiled bleakly. "I'd say no. I'd concede the possibility, of course. He has an aptitude. An almost incredible insight where guns are concerned. Incredible. Because in nothing else . . ."

The words petered out in a puzzled wave of his hand. "That's why I've encouraged it, you understand. It's one thing he seems to grasp. Guns. Cowboys. And naturally, anything that arouses his interest, well, we work on it. Always."

"Would you say Tommy knows right from wrong?"

"Most certainly. He's obedient. Little trouble. Otherwise we couldn't have him here. He'd have to be—put away."

He looked across at his wife who stared back at him a moment then once more returned to her knitting, fiercely absorbed.

Steven was puzzled by the knitting. Her movements were stiff, slow. She pushed the needle through each stitch, carefully looped the wool over, pulled it through. He thought of Kylie laughing and talking, eyes barely glancing at the swiftly moving needles.

Mrs White was not an experienced knitter, he decided, wondered why she thought the camouflage necessary.

"Professor, d'you think Tommy is capable of killing a man?"

Steven, startled by the abruptness of the question, watched

38

White keenly. The other man did not answer immediately, heaved himself to his feet, began pacing up and down the tiled floor.

"I was hoping you wouldn't ask me that question," he said quietly. "Because unfortunately the answer is yes. If—and mind you it is a big 'if'—if someone put a loaded gun in his hand, told him to shoot, he'd shoot it. And if someone got in the way of the bullet—well, yes, I'm afraid he's quite capable of killing a man that way. I have to admit it."

"And if the man fell down dead?"

"But they always do, don't they, Inspector?" He hardly paused in his pacing, deftly catching the question like an interjection at a lecture. "That's one of the first rules of playing cowboy games. The goodie shoots the baddie. The baddie falls down dead."

"And Tommy knows enough for that?"

"Yes, he knows enough for that. Of course, he'd expect the baddie to get up again, go on with the game. And if he didn't, well, Tommy would lose interest. Probably wander off. He—he lacks concentration. His mind . . ."

He paused in the middle of the floor, lines of pain etched deep on his face, a man of sorrows, broken and bleeding for the multitude to see. Suddenly he shook himself, blinked, spoke in a normal voice—and the illusion was gone.

"So you see, Inspector, I have to admit that Tommy is quite capable of killing a man. To Tommy it would be playing a game. And the man would get up and go away when the game was over."

There was silence as he sat down again, faced them with candid eyes.

"You claim Tommy would have to be given a loaded gun?"

"I'm afraid so. Loaded and ready to fire. He does know how to pull a trigger. Most youngsters do. But a fine trigger. Tommy has very little strength in his hands."

Peacock looked at Steven who nodded. "Yes, fairly fine. Almost hair trigger."

The professor looked a trifle disappointed then he shrugged as though half expecting that answer.

39

"This collection of yours. Is Tommy allowed access?"

"When I'm around. That is the rule. And Tommy is good with rules. But he does have two or three guns in his room. No value. Like the one he took down town with him."

"You've got that one back?"

"Yes, thanks. Tommy put it in the letter box. Quite an interesting piece, Inspector. Beautifully decorated but—some vandal got loose on the mechanism, some amateur gunsmith, welded it into a solid mass. Destroyed its value completely."

"So you don't know where he got hold of the Luger?"

"No. Except he says 'they' gave it to him. Whoever 'they' are."

"You've already questioned him?"

White's eyes narrowed. "Of course! Natural, don't you think? Mrs White rang. I came right over. And we tried to find out what it was all about. But we didn't get very far. It's so difficult with Tommy. No straight forward recital, only bits. After a while you learn to fill in the gaps. But we gather he was playing cowboys. He shot a baddie. The baddie was at Mrs Gregg's house. And 'they', 'they' gave him a gun. After that nothing! I'm afraid Tommy's concentration cannot be held for any length of time. Makes it difficult, exhausting, for both him and the questioner."

That, thought Steven, was a pointed reminder that we are not going to learn too much from Tommy even if we try.

"And where is Tommy now?"

"In his room. We knew you'd be around to question him."

"Do you believe Tommy actually fired that shot?"

White fingered his forehead. "No," he said at last. "I've thought about this as carefully as possible. Trying to imagine exactly what happened. And I feel this particular shot was aimed. Had to be. After all, if your constable came across Tommy banging away with a Luger, he'd keep out of the way, wouldn't he?"

Peacock ignored the question. "Well, I'm sorry, but we'll have to question the boy."

White smiled sadly. "Yes. We expected that. We hoped it might be avoided but we do recognize the necessity." He looked at Mrs White. "My dear?" he said softly.

The woman stood obediently, placing her knitting carefully on the table, not looking at Peacock or Steven. "I'll bring him down," she said so quietly they guessed the words rather than heard them.

White sat in his straight-backed chair, silent now, withdrawn. Steven found himself listening to other sounds in the house, a door opening, voices, footsteps on the stairs.

The door opened. Mrs White entered leading Tommy by the hand. He was still wearing his cowboy outfit but the star-studded hat, the tooled boots had been removed. On his feet were a pair of beaded moccasins that made Steven think of an Indian suit somewhere in Tommy's room, minutely perfect in every detail.

Tommy advanced into the room, passed the two police officers, stood in front of his father. White turned him gently.

"These gentlemen want to talk to you, Tommy."

Tommy started playing with the fringe on his cowboy suit, head down, thin fingers busy, until White gave him a light nudge. Tommy moved forward reluctantly to stand awkwardly in front of Peacock.

"Hello, Tommy. Did you see all the excitement to-day?"

He reached forward, pulled the boy closer and, to Steven's surprise, related the whole sequence of the staged robbery as though he had been present.

But the effort was having the desired effect. Tommy lifted his head, dull eyes focused on Peacock's mouth, watching the words come out to build a picture just for him.

Peacock finished dramatically. "But one of them got away, did you know that, Tommy? A gambling man. A real baddie. Got clean away. No one knew where he went. No one!"

Tommy wriggled, the barest touch of animation lifting the slurred voice. "I did, mister. I did. They told me. The hideaway. Wait, they said. And I waited. Waited. And the baddie. The black bandit——" He shaped his fingers into a gun. "Bang! Bang! You're dead. He fell down, mister. Fell down. By the stairs."

"And the gun?" prompted Peacock.

"They promised. Promised. Go to the hideaway. Wait, they said. I waited. Waited. The black bandit——"

Peacock interrupted, "Who are 'they', Tommy?"

Tommy's hand dropped, his attention wavered. He leaned forwards toying with the club button in Peacock's lapel.

Peacock knew when to admit defeat. He pulled out the badge, gave it to Tommy as he talked over his head to White.

"That's as far as you got, I presume, Professor?"

White nodded. " 'Fraid so. Seems the key word is 'they'. As soon as we ask who they are, he dries up."

"Like a form of mental block?"

White stiffened but answered levelly enough. "More or less. Whether it means anything, I can't say. The chances of ever finding out——"

He shook his head, looking down at Tommy seated on the floor. The colours of the emblem seemed to fascinate the boy. He turned it this way and that to catch the light.

Peacock sighed. "Keep working on it. If you manage to get anything more out of him, let us know."

He stood up. "All right, Tommy. We're going now." Tommy looked up at him blankly, hiding his treasure carefully in his hand. Peacock fished a ballpoint from his pocket. "Here, Tommy, like to draw some pictures? Try this pencil. A pretty green one."

Tommy cautiously placed the button on the floor, reached for the pencil. On cue, Mrs White hurried forward with a white scratch pad, placed it on the table.

"Here, Tommy love, here's a nice place to draw."

She settled the boy on a seat at the table while Peacock retrieved his possession from the floor. Deftly she replaced the ballpoint with a coloured pencil, passed the biro back to Peacock.

Leaning over the table, watching Tommy's drawing, she merely nodded when they made their farewells. White came out with them on to the porch, closed the door carefully behind him.

"Inspector, I'd like to thank you," he said gravely. "The way you handled Tommy! He usually ignores strangers. But you had him talking! Quite a feat, I assure you. Obviously, you're used to handling difficult witnesses."

"We are," agreed Peacock. "And don't forget! If he does expand on that 'they' business, let me know."

42

"Then you do think someone else might be involved?"

Peacock paused. "Shall we say that at this stage of the investigation we cannot reject any item of information, however slight or seemingly unrelated."

White nodded slowly, turned away, shoulders even more bowed, stopped when Peacock spoke again.

"Dr White, what would be Tommy's life expectation?"

The hazel eyes narrowed, wary. "Tommy's living on borrowed time, Inspector. Only Mrs White's constant devotion keeps him alive. You've seen him at his best. But when he's ill——" He shook his head, sighed.

"Is Tommy ill very often?" asked Peacock.

"More frequently now. Of course, we were warned it would be like that. The illnesses closer and closer until——" He spread his hands. "It's taking it out of Mrs White though. Not many long spells in between now."

"And these illnesses. Do they strike him suddenly?"

"No. Very gradual. He loses co-ordination. Falters when he walks. Eventually he can do nothing for himself. Lies there only semi-conscious. After a week or so he starts to recover. Sometimes I think she drags him back by sheer willpower."

He watched them tensely, waiting for the next question but Peacock nodded, apparently satisfied. White stayed on the porch, gazing after them as they walked down the narrow path.

At the gateway they paused, surprised to find the footpath crowded by hurrying young men. The technical institute had ended its classes, students were rushing to catch trains, buses.

Peacock grimaced at Steven as together they shouldered their way through to climb into the comparative quiet of the car.

As Steven placed the key in the ignition, Peacock made a restraining gesture. He sat watching the moving crowd while talking to Steven without turning his head.

"How was Tommy holding the Luger when you saw him?"

"Normally. Way anyone would. Anyone playing cowboys."

"Aim it at all?"

"Well, he lifted it at me. Yes, I'd say he aimed it."

Peacock favoured him with a slanting side-glance. "Weren't you worried? It could've been loaded."

"Then someone else would've copped it long before me. He was banging, 'You're dead', all along the street."

"And, of course, it could've been a toy gun?"

"Tommy White doesn't play with toy guns."

Peacock nodded, turned back to his scrutiny of the passing youths. "And you are quite sure he aimed it at you?"

"He aimed it. No one will convince me otherwise."

"I was just wondering. White made such a point of his weak hands. They are weak, fingers anyway. But his wrists seem strong enough. Strong enough to hold a gun and aim it."

He hurriedly wound down the window. "Donald!" he called.

A fair-haired lad stopped by the car. "Hello, Inspector. What're you doing in this neck of the woods?"

"We've been to see Dr White," responded Peacock glibly. "Interesting gun collection he's got there."

"Yes, I'll say," Donald's face lit up. "Did he show you the miniatures? But of course he did. He's nuts about those guns."

"You've seen them?"

"Oh, yes. Whenever we go over to rehearse." He grinned engagingly. "He's nuts on theatre, too, y'know. Just about runs the local repertory. And he's doing a play right now. Dragged some of us in for the mob scenes. Not that we had to be dragged, mind you. Working with the prof., you sort of catch the bug too."

"Head of your department, is he?"

"No. I'm taking engineering. But Lenny—Lenny Stone," he jerked his head towards his stocky friend. "He's got a major rôle so that means we can go to rehearsals together."

"I can imagine. Remember me to your father, will you, Donald. Tell him I'll be around to see him soon."

He watched Donald join his companion, hurry away.

"Donald Pursey. Bright lad. That bit about the repertory. Interesting, don't you think? I'd say Dr White gave a very polished performance."

CHAPTER V

"THIS WAY, PLEASE, gentlemen," said the pretty receptionist. "I'll let Mr Palmer know you are here."

They passed through the tiny reception office into a larger room behind. The girl indicated two chairs, went into the abutting surgery closing the door behind her.

Peacock grimaced sourly at Steven. "She was expecting us. Why?"

Steven shrugged. It seemed that way. They had hardly entered the waiting-room with its small collection of patients when the girl had appeared at the counter. They had moved over to her, Peacock opening his mouth to identify himself but the girl had spoken first. Now they waited for one of the partners of Palmer, Humphrey and Lysaght, Dental Surgeons.

The door opened, a short slender man entered. He spoke briskly, almost belligerently. "Oh, so you're here. I must say I don't like your methods, gentlemen. A 'phone call. Damned cruel to say the least."

"You were expecting us?" asked Peacock.

"Not exactly. Done all the damage, I felt. But, of course, you'd have to do a bit of mopping up, I suppose."

Peacock raised his hand. "Wait a minute, Mr Palmer. Evidently you're expecting the police over some other matter. In actual fact, we came to see Miss Muir, if we may."

"Miss Muir's gone home. Straight away, of course. Took her home myself. Least I could do."

"Straight after what?" asked Peacock patiently.

"After the 'phone call, of course."

'What 'phone call?"

45

Finally it penetrated. "Why, the 'phone call about Joe Blaney. It—it is true, isn't it? He was shot!"

"Yes. He was shot. That's what we came to tell Miss Muir. But it seems someone anticipated us. Any idea who it was?"

"A woman, I think. But we thought it was police."

"It wasn't police. We don't do things that way."

"But this was at least an hour ago!"

"Possible. Blaney was found shot. At three-ten precisely. Since then we've been making inquiries. We intended telling Miss Muir and interviewing her at the same time."

Slightly mollified, Palmer still tried to bluster. "She should've been notified immediately. Immediately!"

Peacock shook his head. "No. Next of kin first. That's the rule. And his father's next of kin. Lives in Auckland."

Palmer was contrite. "Sorry. Sorry. I'm afraid I've been blaming you for unnecessary callousness when——"

Peacock waved the apology aside. "You took Miss Muir home, you say. And left her alone?"

"No. Her flat mate's there. Judy Clark. We checked."

"How did she take it? Miss Muir, I mean."

"Fainted. Rather disconcerting, to say the least. Several patients waiting and everything. Saw it all."

"Who took the 'phone call?"

Miss Adams stepped forward. "I did. Arline, Miss Muir, was making out appointment cards. In here. The woman didn't identify herself. Just asked for Miss Muir. I called Arline then a patient came in. I was attending to him when I heard Arline say, 'Oh,' then—well, she fainted."

"Leaving the 'phone off the hook?"

"Yes. I think she did. But I ran for Mr Palmer."

"That's right, Inspector. I went out and picked Miss Muir up, brought her in here. Of course, we didn't know what it was all about. Not till she came round." Palmer coughed. "I'm afraid I replaced the 'phone, Inspector. Did it without thinking."

"Well, Miss Muir was your first concern," said Peacock quietly. "Did she cry much?"

"Why, no. She didn't cry. Kind of frozen. Voice dead. Y'know. Just sat there staring into space."

"Yes. Seen it before. Still, we have to talk to her. D'you mind letting Miss Clark know we're coming."

"We'll do that for you, Inspector," said Palmer nodding at Miss Adams. "You know the address?"

"We know the address." They left the office as Miss Adams was dialling, went out into the afternoon sunshine.

"So someone got in ahead of us," said Peacock as Steven started the car. "Who d'you think the woman was? Mrs Gregg?"

"Must've been. Think she'd have a bit more sense. Wonder what she thought when Muir flaked out on her."

"Delighted, I'd say. If she'd been in the least bit concerned, she'd have rung back."

Steven stole a side glance at his superior, noted the dark look on his face. Old Jonas did not like Mrs Gregg, for all her daintiness and pretty affectations.

The High Street address turned out to be a shop with the flat at the top of a narrow stairway. The two men paused on the dark landing, blinked at the bright orange door lit by a shaft of sunlight filtering through the grimy skylight.

Peacock lifted his hand to knock, hesitated, tilted his head, listened. From inside came the sound of music, slow, mournful, tearing at the soul. He raised an eyebrow at Steven. "All right. You're the expert. What is it?"

"Greig. *The Last Spring*. Royal Philharmonic."

"Music to be melancholy by, eh?" He allowed his knuckles to drop softly against the door panel, waited, knocked again.

The door opened. Judy Clark stood there, black hair brushed primly back, brown eyes mildly inquiring. The professional empty smile deepened, she nodded, opened the door wider.

Through the white box of a hall, they entered the main room, chromatic with harsh blues, reds, broad bands of black.

Steven was not surprised. After that orange door he had been prepared for anything.

Judy waited in the centre of the room, watching their faces. "Listen," she said, indicating the half-closed door on her right.

They listened, feeling the morbid music wash over them in a prickling stream.

47

"Arline," said Judy quietly. "Thinks it's appropriate for the occasion. They gave her brandy. Made her quite maudlin."

"D'you think—" began Peacock, coughed when he realized he was whispering, spoke again in a more normal voice. "D'you think it's wise?"

Judy shrugged. "Won't hurt her. Has to get it out of her system. Why not this way?"

"We'd like to speak to her," said Peacock. "Now!"

"You're welcome. If you can break through. I'll let her know you're here."

"Wait a minute. Didn't they ring you?"

Judy stopped, turned to face them. "Why, yes. They rang. I told Arline then. Tried to. But she was too—well, immersed in this."

She walked across the striped carpet to the white door, shoulders square, confident. She knocked lightly, entered the room.

Steven and Peacock heard the sound of her voice, soft at first, then louder, sharper. Silence. Judy came back into the room, leaned against the door, hands behind her.

She shook her head. "No soap! Can't get through at all."

She came further into the room. "Y'know, I thought it might be all right. But she's retreated so much. Maybe the wrong thing after all."

She stood there rubbing one hand against the other, a puzzled look in her brown eyes.

"Maybe I can help," said Peacock, stepping forward.

"No! It wouldn't do any good. You'd better come back later." She looked up to encounter Peacock's hard stare. Her eyes wavered. She moved aside.

Peacock pushed the door wide, stood for a moment surveying the room. The venetian blinds were closed, dim light barely showing the figure of Arline Muir lying on the divan bed, hands clasped loosely in front of her, eyes staring at the ceiling.

Peacock sighed, went over to the record-player, turned it off. The figure on the bed moaned, lifted a weary hand in protest. He turned to the window, opened the slats of the blind. The late afternoon sun streamed in, warm and wholesome.

Arline rolled away from the light, flung a protective arm over her eyes. "Leave me. Leave me alone."

Peacock leaned over her. "Not exactly the way I'd expect a policeman's girl to act," he sneered. "Thought you'd have more guts."

Arline sat up abruptly, looked angry enough to make some acid retort. Instead she wilted suddenly, her whole body sagging into pathetic helplessness.

"You don't know. You don't know how it feels."

"You'd be surprised," responded Peacock, settling in the small basket chair by the side of the bed. "Now, Miss Muir. We know you've had a nasty shock. But it would be better for you to talk about it. You're not helping Joe by giving in like this. You're not helping yourself. And we need to talk to you—now!"

Arline swallowed with difficulty, looked squarely at Peacock. "Yes, you're right," she said gravely. "I'm not behaving very well, am I? I suppose you've seen plenty of the bereft, and they've all behaved quite calmly, quite naturally."

She gave a bitter laugh as she manoeuvred to sit on the edge of the bed facing Peacock, legs tucked demurely underneath, delicately balanced like a drooping flower.

"How can I help?" she asked wanly.

As Peacock began the routine questioning, Steven studied the girl's face. There were no signs of weeping, grey eyes clear behind dark lashes, soft mouth tranquil under pale lipstick. Freshly applied lipstick. Steven had a momentary vision of Arline seated in front of the mirror, carefully enhancing the pallor of her face, outlining her lips, into a bleached presentation of the vivid photograph on Joe Blaney's bedside table. He wondered idly if she had done it before or after Judy had warned her they were coming.

"Did he ever mention being threatened?"

Arline brushed a wayward hair from her eyes, gazed soulfully at Peacock before answering in a hushed voice.

"Yes, Inspector. He'd even been attacked. Just before he came down here."

"This was at Taupo?"

She nodded, dropping her lids to veil the curiously avid gleam in her eyes. Steven interposed sharply.

"An accident, sir. Constable Blaney was involved in a car accident at Taupo. Isn't that so, Miss Muir."

The barest flicker of irritation crossed her face, she shrugged, remained silent. Peacock waited patiently for an answer but she ignored him.

"Did Blaney at any time claim it was not an accident, Miss Muir?" He had to repeat the question before her attention lifted long enough from her fingers to answer with a reluctant "No".

"Then why——?" Peacock stopped, realizing this was not the time, began again. "All right. We'll try something else. This Ponderosa Day. The bank robbery. You knew Blaney was going to be one of the bandits?"

"No. We weren't supposed to know, were we?"

"You weren't supposed to know but Blaney being your fiancé, I thought maybe——"

"Joe never discussed his cases with me. With anyone. Except perhaps when they were over. Then maybe he'd tell us, me, a bit more than appeared in the papers."

"So you didn't know what arrangements had been made."

"No."

Peacock studied the girl for a long silent minute, lifted an eyebrow at Steven, stood up to leave and Arline pounced.

"Wait!" she cried wildly. "I was told—they said it was an accident."

Peacock nodded. "It looks like an accident."

"Then why all this—questioning?"

"We have to investigate every angle, Miss Muir."

Arline thought this over, shook her head, lay back on the bed. "They said it was an accident," she said flatly, eyes once more fixed on the ceiling. "An accident."

As Steven closed the door gently, Judy Clark turned to face them. She had been sitting by the window gazing down into the street, face serene, a picture of quiet efficiency despite the cigarette burning unheeded between her fingers.

"Is she all right?" she asked.

"I think so," said Peacock. "Now, we'd like to ask you a few questions."

"Yes. I was afraid of that. Take a pew." She ground out the cigarette in an ash tray shaped like a hospital utensil.

"How long have you known Joe Blaney?"

"Oh, about three months. Thereabouts."

"Since Arline started going with him? And you started going with Lance Brendon?"

"Well, I'm not exactly going with Lance." She emphasized the word with a slight moue. "I make up the foursome, that's all."

"Miss Muir was engaged to Joe Blaney?"

"More or less. I think Joe wanted her to meet his father first. Before it was official, I mean. They were going to Auckland over Christmas. His father's a policeman, y'know."

Peacock nodded. "Did he ever mention his police work?"

"Joe?" Judy smiled. "No. He took his job very seriously. I'd say he lived very much by the book, did our Joe."

"But you knew he was going to be a bandit to-day."

"Oh, yes," she said frankly then paused, sensing something in the phrasing of the question. "Oh, fell into that one, didn't I? Arline said we didn't, I suppose. Good old loyal Arline. Standing guard on a dead man's reputation. Quite in the best tradition, what!"

Her flippancy surprised Steven and perhaps she guessed their reaction because her voice was more subdued when she continued.

"Actually, Lance told us. Joe was furious. But Lance, of course, well, it was a game to him. Said it wouldn't hurt a couple more knowing. We'd keep it quiet for Joe's sake. Anyway, I don't think it mattered all that much. We still wouldn't be able to say what he was wearing. For the bounty thing, I mean."

"So you never saw his costume?"

"No. I understand Mr Cottar made all the arrangements. Hired the costumes and so on. Don't think even Joe knew exactly what he was going to wear."

"No fittings?"

51

"No. Mean too many would know about it, y'see. Besides they didn't have to fit all that well."

"When did Blaney collect his costume?"

"Just before, the way I heard it. They—the bandits—went up to Cottars, changed, then Mr Cottar brought them down to a pre-arranged spot to the horses. All very hush, hush, y'know."

"How did Blaney get up to Cottars?"

"Lance took him. About quarter-to-one, I think."

"In the patrol car?"

"No. His own car. An old Standard. Had quite a busy morning, I believe. Running around. Messages and so on for the committee. Volunteered his services, believe it or not." The sneer that accompanied these words suggested how out of character that was.

"You're sure he didn't use the patrol car?"

"Sure I'm sure. He couldn't get permission. Oh, he had official permission to ferry Joe home all right. Part of the co-operation bit between departments. But nix on taking him up to Cottars. Couldn't see the difference, myself. But the departmental mind, well, y'know."

"Miss Clark, who told you about the shooting?"

"Why, Lance rang. He knew I'd be home. At least, hoped so. Warned me Arline might be coming home early. Y'know, in case I was thinking of going out on a shopping spree or something."

"You know the details then?"

"All that he could tell me."

"Did you know Tommy White?"

Judy shrugged. "Depends on what you mean by 'know'. I've seen him around, if you know what I mean. And, of course, I know the—circumstances."

"Were you surprised to learn he was involved?"

Judy thought about that. "Yes. I think so. Yes. I was very surprised. Although one can never be absolutely sure, can one?"

Nothing they asked Judy told them anything further so Peacock and Steven made their departure, set off in the direction of Jeff Cottar's.

"Wonder where Gregg was at lunch time?" Peacock said as they raced through the evening traffic.

"Gregg?" wondered Steven. "On the beach, wasn't he?"

"He says. He also says he saw Blaney in the patrol car dressed in his gambler's outfit. That had to be some time before two. It also had to be some place between the pub and Gregg's place. North of Jackson Street. The beach is south. So, where was Mr Gregg? Not down on the beach anyway. Wonder why he thought it necessary to lie?"

CHAPTER VI

COTTAR'S HOME WAS set below the eastern hills. Steven followed Peacock under an archway dripping with crimson ramblers, sauntered along the wide drive appreciating the smooth lawn, carefully-tended flower beds and shrubs.

"Someone has green fingers," muttered Peacock.

"Gardener probably. Cottar pulled himself up by his boot-straps and now he's got it, he has all the trimmings."

Steven regretted such trimmings as the fluted sandstone columns on the entrance patio but succumbed to the gracious elegance of the hallway revealed by the half-open door.

He was about to ring the bell when a small girl dressed in cowgirl costume tumbled into view. She surveyed them with solemn inquiring eyes which suddenly brightened.

"D'you want to see Beerpop?" she asked pertly.

Mildly amused, Steven answered gravely, "We'd like to see Mr Cottar. I believe he's expecting us."

The child laughed. "I'll tell him. I'll tell Beerpop," she cried, swung to scamper away from their sight. There was a sound of collision, a soft voice inquired, "What's the matter, Mylene?"

They did not hear the child's reply but, the next instant, a tall fair-haired girl stepped into the hallway.

"Oh," she said quietly. "You're the police, aren't you? Dad told me you were coming. Will you come this way, please."

She preceded them to a compact office leading off the side passage.

"If you'll wait here, I'll give him a call."

Indicating two chairs, she dialled, spoke briefly over the desk telephone. "He won't be long. The factory's just in the next street."

The tiny girl had moved over to lean against Steven's knee. "You want to see Beerpop?" she demanded again, gazing into his face.

Steven looked over her head at the woman who smiled as she explained. "A family name. For Dad—Mr Cottar. Mylene's his grand-daughter. Whenever Dad comes over to visit, well, my husband more often than not says, 'Have a beer, Pop?' Mylene's called him that ever since she could talk. Thinks it's his name."

The two men laughed, Mylene giggling uncertainly in unison. Steven leaned forward. "You make a pretty cowgirl, Mylene. Can you ride a horse?"

Mylene shook her pony tail. "No. But Beerpop can. He's a Nited States marshal."

She would have continued chattering but her mother shushed her gently at the sound of a far door closing.

"Come along, Mylene. We're in the way here." She swooped the child into her arms, was outside the small office before the bulk of Cottar's figure filled the doorway.

He had discarded the gunbelt, the wide-brimmed hat, still looked formidably official in the dark-blue marshal's outfit with outsize silver star.

"Nasty business," he said as he manoeuvred himself around to the back of his desk. "Now, exactly how can I help?"

"I think you'd better give us a rundown on this Ponderosa Day set-up first. How it was arranged and so forth."

Cottar pursed his lips in concentration. "You know the bit about Anderson saying Petone looked like a scene from a bad TV western? And you know we decided to cash in on the publicity?"

At Peacock's nod, he continued. "Well, we set up a committee. Had a kind of brain-storm meeting for ideas. And we had plenty of those, believe you me. Including the staged robbery. Felt it wouldn't be authentic without one."

"D'you remember who made that particular suggestion?"

"Nooo. It just came up. Quite frankly, we were all getting quite a kick out of, well, playing cowboys and indians again. And we didn't have too much time. Ten days from go to whoa.

So we all pitched in with ideas, practically non-stop. But who exactly suggested what, well, beyond me."

"Probably not important. Now, about the robbery itself."

"Well, in a thing like this we had to have the co-operation of the police, you understand, and Bob Duffy, he's the sec-retary . . ." He paused. "Y'know, I think he's the one who threw in that idea. Manager of the Enzed, y'know, the bank we robbed. Yes, I'm certain now. His idea all right, because we knew which bank straight away. Didn't have to ask anyone's permission or anything."

"Sounds reasonable."

"Yes. Bob Duffy. As I was saying, he was detailed to approach the police. See what you thought about it. Sergeant Fairbrother, that is. A bit wary about it at first."

"Naturally. We've had one or two unhappy experiences of late. A bank robbery used to be one of those things that just didn't happen in New Zealand. But lately there seems to be quite a rash of them and your scheme, well, it was just asking for some smart alec to take over."

"Y'think so? Myself, I thought we were moving a mite too fast for anything like that to happen. Still, you're the professionals. Know what you're talking about. And we appreciated that, agreed to all the police conditions. Y'know, clearing the bank of all unauthorized personnel ten minutes before, locking the tellers' drawers, so on and so forth."

"Did you pick Blaney?"

"No. We left that to the sergeant. Only stipulation we made: he had to be able to ride. Not just sit a horse but really ride."

"Who picked the others?"

"I did. And Bob Duffy. We got together, worked it out be-tween us. Y'see that bit had to be secret. Because of the bounty."

"So, on the arranging side, only you and Duffy knew Blaney was involved. And the other three bandits."

"Yes. They knew. We had a couple of rehearsals."

He grinned remembering. "Had to. Get the timing right. Without the horses, of course. Not in town either. Down on the old tip road. We measured out the equivalent area, worked out a sort of script."

"And you personally arranged for the costumes."

"That's right. Hired them from repertory. One gambler's outfit, three cowboy. Tried to get another gambler but that's all they had."

"Who decided Blaney should be the gambler?"

Cottar shook his head. "No one really. The boys were all much the same size. Blaney maybe an inch taller, a stone heavier. I just shoved the costumes in the locker room, let them take their pick."

"In the factory? Your factory personnel saw them?"

"No." Cottar smiled. "Most of our work's outside. Just do a bit of prefab—lining-up inside the factory. This afternoon everyone was on outside jobs."

"How did Blaney arrive?"

Cottar shrugged. "Can't say for sure but probably by car. I asked them to come separately so no one would see the four of them together at any time."

"Wouldn't the neighbours see? Guess they were the bandits?"

"Doubtful. This was campaign headquarters. People coming and going all day. Mostly in western costume. Anyway, the only time they were bandits was when they were wearing the hair. Y'know, moustaches and such. Then I smuggled them into the car through the loading bay—and three of them back again after."

"Right. Well, we'll have to interview these men, of course. If you'd give me their names and addresses."

"No need. I've got them waiting. Rounded them up as soon as I heard. Won't be a sec." He picked up the telephone, dialled, gave terse instructions. "Yes. This is it. Come straight up to the house, all of you. They won't be long," he said as he replaced the telephone, settled back into his chair.

"The celebrations pretty well over now?" asked Peacock.

"Not quite. A concert to-night at half-past seven." Instinctively he glanced at the clock. "About an hour from now. Country-and-western songs from a well-known group. Barn dancing in the street. We're closing that area off again for the final bit. Finish about ten, I think."

He paused, tapping the newspaper on the desk. "As a matter of fact, I thought this might put a damper on things but maybe

57

people won't notice. Not exactly spread across the paper, is it? Very discreet. No mention of Tommy. No connection with Ponderosa Day. Just a bald statement. 'Policeman found shot.' "

"We wanted to make the evening edition. Get that bit about the gun in front of the public."

"You're hoping someone will come forward with the right kind of information?"

"That's the general idea. D'you know of anyone?"

Cottar shook his head. "Hand guns? One or two. Bank property. Not easily accessible. Not a Luger, though. Wonder where Tommy got that."

"Could've helped himself."

"Perhaps." Cottar frowned, stared at the floor. "Funny that Tommy knew about Blaney. Going back to Gregg's, I mean. Must've been waiting for him."

"Must've been."

They paused, looked towards the door as three big men crowded into the small office, draped themselves around the room. They all looked sheepish, all smelled convivially of beer.

"John Goodman. Bill Foster. Hugh McNeely." Cottar reeled off the names, pointing to each in turn.

Peacock looked each man over slowly. "You know what you're here for, don't you?" he asked blandly.

"Yeh," said McNeely, deep-voiced, solemn-faced. "Yeh. Jeff told us. About the shooting. And little Tommy."

Peacock looked at Cottar as though wondering exactly what he had told them. Naturally they would have discussed the news, decided amongst themselves what to say. He waited quietly for someone to speak.

McNeely had apparently been elected spokesman. He cleared his throat after a definite nudge from Foster. "Happened while we were finishing off the play bit, seems like. Jeff collected us, brought us back here. To change, y'see. All together till after three, I guess."

Peacock glanced at Steven, smiled thinly. He might have expected something like that but he was not particularly interested.

"Any of you men own guns?" he asked abruptly.

McNeely nodded. "Two. Rifle. Shotgun."

58

Foster and Goodman also owned hunting guns, Foster adding that he belonged to a small bore club, was the reigning Hutt Valley champion.

"Anyone own a hand gun?" When the three men shook their heads, he continued. "Ever used one?"

The men began to shuffle their feet, look uncomfortable. Foster said a trifle belligerently, "I've shot a Biretta, Inspector. Had one on the other side. Didn't bring it back with me though. Knew you'd take it off me."

Peacock nodded. "It is customary. Know anyone who owns a Luger?"

"Bob Duffy, I think," said McNeely doubtfully. "A hand gun anyway."

"No one else?"

The men looked uninterested. No one spoke.

"You knew Blaney was going to duck out the way he did?"

"Sure," from McNeely. "Thought it was a good idea. Make it a bit harder, y'see."

"Who made the suggestion? D'you remember?"

McNeely moved uneasily. "Guess I did. Kind of. Confuse the public. Y'see. And Joe was a natural. A policeman. More conspicuous than any of the rest of us. I mean, when he got back on to the street."

"Did you discuss this with anyone else?"

"I didn't. Fact is, that side of it was left to Joe and Lance. Worked it out between them."

Peacock looked at the other men who shook their heads. "Not even with your wives?"

Foster laughed. "Particularly not with our wives."

"Foster," said Peacock crisply. "Your wife knew you were to be one of the bandits, didn't she? For instance, you did go to rehearsals."

"I went to committee meetings, Inspector. And I think the same with everyone else. I mean, if my wife knew, and John's, and Hugh's—well, they're friends. We had to keep our mouths shut."

"And Blaney? D'you think he was so discreet?"

Foster shrugged. "Well, in his case, maybe the whole police

59

force. Way it was done. The police had to provide a bandit. He had to be able to ride, real good. So maybe they asked around. Got Joe Blaney. Then there was some alteration to his duty roster, I understand. So he could be at rehearsals."

"Right. We'll leave it at that. We know where to get in touch if we need you." The three men looked like children let out of school, started to troop out of the room.

In the doorway, McNeely paused, turned back. "Inspector," he said diffidently. "Did Tommy White really shoot Joe Blaney?"

"It looks that way."

"But Tommy White! I just can't believe it. Why, he's—he's——" He stopped, groping for the words he wanted.

"Harmless?" supplied Peacock. "No one's entirely harmless. Not with a loaded gun in his hand."

"But Tommy White! It was an accident, wasn't it? Had to be. Couldn't be anything else!" He paused, watching Peacock's eyes. He was not reassured by what he saw there. A look of contempt twisted his face. "Of course, Blaney's a cop. That's it, isn't it? You've got to sacrifice someone. Make 'em respect the law, eh? Even a poor little bastard like Tommy White."

He choked on the bitter words. Peacock dropped his eyes, looked sideways at Cottar who was signalling at McNeely to keep quiet.

He looked back at McNeely. "Of course, we've considered the possibility that Tommy is merely a cover. That means someone gave him a gun. Told him where to find Blaney. Someone who knew the set-up in detail. Like you, for instance. And," he continued silkily, "weren't you the one who actually suggested Blaney should do this ducking out bit?"

McNeely stiffened. His mouth hardened. "I'm in the clear, mister," he said coldly. "Don't you think you can pin this one on me." He pivoted on his heel, disappeared after his companions.

Peacock turned to Cottar who was carefully scrutinizing the paper in front of him.

"There's someone else," he said mildly. "Your deputy."

Cottar snapped to attention. "Tony Gerrard. A ring in. Last

minute. I talked him into being deputy, gave him a rough idea what to do and he just followed me."

"Didn't you have a deputy planned?"

"Oh, yes, Jimmy Clausen. But his father died suddenly. Had to go home. Hamilton, I think. Got the address here some-where." He flicked the telstat on his desk, ran a finger down the page. "No. Sorry. But Bob Duffy knows. I'll get him to ring."

"Thanks. And we'll get Hamilton police on the job. See if he talked to anyone." He stood up, glanced at Steven.

"Is that all, gentlemen?" asked Cottar hopefully.

"For now, Mr Cottar," said Peacock. "We may need your assistance again later."

Cottar walked with them to the front door. "You'll find we'll be as co-operative as possible, Inspector. All of us. We're just as interested in getting this cleared up as you are. Because Blaney's death, well, it's spoiled things for everyone."

At the door, Peacock halted, faced Cottar squarely. "D'you think Tommy White killed Joe Blaney?" he asked abruptly.

Cottar shrugged. "An accident. Like Hugh said. Accidents can happen to anyone."

"Tommy was waiting at Gregg's for Blaney to show up. With a gun. Does that sound like an accident, Mr Cottar?"

Cottar's face tightened. "Not that part of it, Inspector. But the rest. If Tommy did fire the actual shot—"

"Well, he says he did. Says he shot the bad man. The bad man fell off the stairs. Isn't that correct?"

"That's what he said. But Tommy—difficult. You're not going to get anything there."

Peacock looked at him curiously. "How can you be so sure? Hard to understand, I grant you. And he hasn't told us very much yet, I agree. But he will. Just a matter of perseverance."

"You think so? You honestly think Tommy will tell you what actually happened?"

"He'll tell us. We'll know soon enough." The tone of quiet confidence evidently impressed Cottar.

"Yes, Inspector, I believe you will. I only said that because we tried to get through to him. Believe you me, we tried. And we got no place. No place at all."

He stood by the fluted pillars, watched them walk down the drive.

"Talk about a closed shop," growled Peacock as he settled into the car. "Nobody wants to believe Tommy White committed murder. An accident, says McNeely. Cottar. Yet Whittaker says no, not an accident. Then rules out Tommy White completely."

"Brendon believes he did it."

"Ah, yes, Brendon. He does believe it, doesn't he? Accepts it anyway. No reason for the killing therefore has to be someone like Tommy White. Not a local man though, is he?"

"No. Comes from New Plymouth. Down here a year or so."

"Thought so. And if someone else is involved, if, it has to be someone like that. Someone who expected the police to accept the face picture. Tommy White got a gun. Tommy White killed a bandit."

"Someone told him where to find Blaney. Someone gave him gun——"

Peacock grunted. "Well, he certainly procured a gun from somewhere. Whether he was given it or not we have yet to prove. And once we know that, or even a bit more about the gun—"

"D'you really think we'll get anything out of Tommy?"

"Do you? I was thinking when we were talking to that little girl back there. How old would she be? Three? Four?"

"Something like that."

"Well, look at the way she was chattering. You could hold an adult conversation with her. Easily. If you asked her who gave her the gun she'd say Beerpop or whoever. She wouldn't say 'they promised' then start playing with a button. Besides, would anything Tommy says be admissible evidence? Could be saying one thing, meaning something entirely different."

"He could still give us a lead. Where to look."

Peacock pulled thoughtfully at his lower lip.

"White said if someone gave Tommy a gun, told him to shoot it, he'd shoot. Someone? Anyone?"

Steven hesitated. "Not just anyone. Someone he was used to maybe."

"So 'they' means someone close to him. Providing the word 'they' means anything. Could be a plant."

"A plant?"

"Yes. By Dr White. What better way to protect Tommy than by making us think someone else is involved. Might even be right. But he's nudging a bit hard, don't you think?"

"Tommy talked about 'they' too, remember."

"That's right. After White had a go at him. Did he mention 'they' when you questioned him?"

"He didn't mention anything. Didn't open his mouth. Just glowered. And when we kept at it began to whimper."

"Then Collins stepped in. Advised you to stop the questioning?"

"That's right."

"Yes," said Peacock thoughtfully. "That's exactly right."

CHAPTER VII

THE LOCAL POLICE station used to be the court house. In 1952, the justice department decided it was redundant, modern travel facilities making Lower Hutt easily available to Petone litigants. In November of that year, police personnel and equipment moved from their cramped quarters close by, spread through the mid-Victorian structure.

Steven drove into the semi-circle of the truncated drive, stopped at the wide grey steps. He followed Peacock into the building, entered the office set aside for their use while the inspector went to consult Senior Sergeant Fairbrother.

The office had probably been a robing room, or a consulting room, the fine panelling showing behind tiers of filing cabinets. Two deal tables, each with a typewriter and four chairs, completed the décor.

Steven found a stack of reports piled on the table facing the door. He sat down, commenced to study them.

Most were routine, uninformative on the surface so Steven contented himself with the usual procedure of underlining times in red, names in green. If Peacock looked through them, the vital information was readily discernible, but he expected to see a summary of information with references back to the original report.

Steven had barely finished the analysis, his own report still in the machine, when Peacock came back.

"Phew!" he said, throwing his hat at the peg on the back of the door. "Making enough row, aren't they?"

Steven smiled indulgently. "Yes. Got the amplifiers right up. Or maybe we're a bit close. Next street, y'know."

Peacock went over to the window, listened to the sounds of

music, laughter, coming from Jackson Street, shut the window.

"Dancing now, by the sound of things. Who are they? The group, I mean."

"The Four Brads. Tops in country and western. They certainly know how to belt it out."

Peacock nodded, seated himself. "Well, it's nice to know something's going right. Anything here?"

Steven handed over his analysis but Peacock placed it on the table without a glance, waited.

"Nothing much. Mostly routine. Did you know Inspector Blaney's coming down on the late plane?"

"Yes. Pal of Fairbrother's. Staying with him. Hoped to have something for him but——"

"You mean away from Tommy White?"

"More or less." He looked at Steven sourly. "Yeh, I know. More dramatic and all that. This way's kind of flat." He fingered his chin. "There was some publicity about the Blaneys, seem to remember. Father and son bit. Public press, I think, but it might've been the *Journal*."

"This it?" asked Steven.

He opened Blaney's photograph album, pushed it towards Peacock. The inspector examined the newspaper clipping taped to the inside cover. It showed Joe Blaney with an older, thinner man, both in uniform. The caption burbled about son following in father's footsteps, chief inspector at Auckland and constable at Napier.

"Yes. That's it. Anything more in this?" His fingers flicked the edge of the small album.

"Nothing relevant. Usual family stuff. Assortment of attractive females. Played around or owned a boat for some time—the *Rosella*. Did a bit of skin diving, skiing, played for police against post office. Otherwise——"

Peacock nodded, said nothing.

"They found the key," said Steven abruptly.

"Oh? Where you suggested?"

"Yes. Buried under the hydrangea. Thought those marigolds might mean something."

"Well, that proves Tommy had the key. What that gives us, I don't know. Find any more bullets?"

"No. Not yet anyway. And the trajectory, almost horizontal with a one degree downward."

Peacock stared at him, pulled a face. "So much for Tommy White. Y'know, I tried to fit him in. Had him dragging that table over. The hydrangea'd screen him so Blaney wouldn't spot him till he was on the stairs. Now——Wait a minute, what if Tommy was on the stairs, shot him through the treads as he came around the side of the house?"

"Means he'd have to hump the body to where it was found. Can't see Tommy doing that. Not strong enough. Then there's the ricochet scar to explain, the blood on the stair."

"Matched it yet."

"No report so far. But it has to be Blaney's."

Peacock drywashed his face. "So, the sink bench——A shot from the fanlight would be exactly right but I can't see Tommy going into the house . . .

His voice trailed off into thoughtful musing. Steven remained silent. He knew when he was being used as a sounding board for ideas, when Peacock was simply thinking aloud.

Peacock sprang to his feet, began pacing up and down the narrow area of floor space. "So what have we got? Tommy White snaffles a gun from somewhere, goes down to Gregg's at exactly the right moment, lifts the key from the cistern, enters the house, climbs on to the sink, waits till Blaney arrives, shoots him through the fanlight, climbs down, locks the back door, buries the key, goes back up town. Tommy White? I don't believe it!"

"You're beginning to sound like Dr Whittaker."

Jonas slumped back into the chair, stared at the ceiling. Steven waited, started re-reading his incomplete report in search of something he had missed.

The older man's fingers strayed to his jacket pocket, took out a wrapper, opened it, placed a pellet on his tongue, began to roll it meditatively around his mouth.

"Not a single solitary soul witnessed anything. No one saw anyone come, anyone leave."

"Everyone was up town. Everyone in that area."

'Yes. Even that Mrs Thingmebob. Bedridden for years, according to Mrs Gregg."

"Mrs Davidson. Not bedridden. Arthritic. Doesn't move around much. Doesn't go out either. Except when transport is provided. The young people haven't a car."

"Convenient, eh? Getting her out of the house?"

"Very. One of the locals thought so, too. Knows the old lady well. A bit difficult. Probably wouldn't have moved if it hadn't been for the old identity competition."

"Oh? Something to entice her out, you mean?"

"Yes. The oldest identity. And Mrs Davidson was it. Quite a write-up in the women's pages." He handed over a clipping for Peacock's perusal. "Personal interview and all that. But she had to be there. Chairs set up by the post office. For the senior citizens."

"Whose suggestion?"

"Can't pin it down. But we know the driver of the car that took her and her grand-daughter down to the post office." He paused, looked at Peacock, smiled grimly. "Traffic Officer Lance Brendon. He also took down the next-door neighbours."

"Very thorough, wasn't he? Any reason?"

"He says, well, he says Blaney had to get back to the flat without being spotted."

"And the old lady spends most of her time at the window, watching the world go by?"

"That's right. Anyway, when he heard about this oldest identity bit, Brendon personally talked Mrs Davidson into entering, volunteered to provide transport."

"Interesting. What about transport back?"

"All arranged but not Brendon. Had to go on duty. A few minutes late anyway. Which is why he dropped Blaney at the gate."

"And he did use the patrol car?"

"To bring Blaney back, yes. Used his own car to take Blaney to Cottars, came back, ferried Mrs Davidson, etc., back again to change then up town for the robbery bit."

"You've confirmed he had permission to use the patrol car?"

"Yes. That was all settled beforehand."

"So transport department also knew Blaney was to be a bandit.

Some of them anyway. Rate we're going everyone in Petone knew." Peacock snorted in disgust.

Soothingly, Steven tried to change the topic. "No way of fitting this Collins thing in?" he asked.

Peacock roused himself. "Can't see it. Fairbrother says Blaney claimed some progress but no proof as yet. Far as he could see Blaney was covering the same ground mostly."

"Need to, wouldn't he? To get the feel of it. Still, Collins wouldn't necessarily know that."

"On the face of it, Collins wouldn't know anything. Officially, it's being handled by Burton. Officially, it's dead. But when Blaney was posted to Petone, Fairbrother thought he'd get some undercover stuff out of him. No loyalties to cloud his thinking."

He swung the chair round, straddled it, began to drum his fingers on the back. "This is the set-up. Eight burglaries over a period of twenty months. Last one four months ago. Small stuff, mostly electrical, jewellery, anything about pocket size."

"Why not shop lifting?"

"No. They proved it happened after the shops closed, before they opened in the morning. Couple of cases had the time down to a few hours. For instance, chap took his wife and daughter to the ballet, came back to Petone, worked in the shop till ten, picked up wife and daughter. On the way home stopped outside the shop to show them the window display. That's when he spotted it."

Steven nodded. "Couldn't get much closer. Much taken?"

"Pocket transistors. Five of them. Three from the window. Two from a display stand inside."

"And other small stuff ignored?"

"Yes. Never more than a couple of handfuls."

"A man walking. Fills his pocket, walks out."

"A man walking, yes. A policeman on the beat. Someone no one would question if he tried a shop door."

"The man on the beat being Collins."

"The man always being Collins."

He grinned wolfishly. "But listen to this. That particular night, half of Gracefield went up in flames. So Collins was very oc-

68

cupied from the time he came on duty till two-thirty in the morning."

Steven remembered that night. One of the most spectacular fires in that area. Discovered shortly after six in one of the pre-fabricated MOW depots, it had already spread to neighbouring quanset-type storehouses, engineering shops, by the time the first fire engine arrived. Drums of diesel oil, swarf, and other highly inflammable items fed the flames till finally overcome by the combined assault of all local brigades.

"So no policeman on duty in Jackson Street!"

Peacock looked at him levelly. "Not officially. But there was a policeman there. Or someone dressed as a policeman. The shop-owner saw him checking doors along the street."

"Ah," said Steven. "That's where the policeman bit came in? Not been able to identify him yet?"

"No. That's why I said someone dressed as a policeman. Could be. Official personnel all accounted for. Not only Petone. Moera, the Bays, Lower Hutt."

"I see. How did he get in?"

"Walked in. Seems like. A key for certain. No sign of break-ing and entering. Except once. Door looked as though it had been forced. Then the owner admitted the lock was stiff. Had to force his way in most mornings, especially after a wet."

"And it always happened when Collins was on nights."

"It only happened when Collins was on nights. Fairbrother says he doesn't like suspecting his own officers but—"

"But Collins was suspended!"

Peacock's eyes glinted. "Oh, been chatting with the boys, have you?"

"Well, not exactly. They were talking Blaney. Someone said worst thing happened around here since Collins was suspen-ded."

"And?"

"I asked all innocent why Collins was suspended but he shut up. Got dumb all of a sudden. I didn't pursue the matter. Decided I'd hear more about it later."

Peacock nodded. "Yes. Collins was suspended. Reinstated after the inquiry. Proved unequivocally he was not involved in

69

at least two cases. Enough to suggest he had nothing to do with the others."

"What was the other one? The other confirming case?"

"Jeweller had a new line of digital watches on display. Went to a church meeting that night. Stopped off at the shop on the way home. Was in the act of opening up when he heard a smash down near the beach."

"Must've been some smash!"

"It was. You'll remember when that tanker cleaned up the Eastbourne bus. Nobody killed but nearly all the passengers were badly hurt."

"Yes. Doctors reckon if that chap hadn't been on the scene so quickly—That your shop-owner?"

"That's right. Head of the local chapter of St John. As soon as he heard the crash, he got weaving. Ran back to his car, dashed down straight away. And get this. He picked Collins up on the way. Collins was running towards the beach. And they were all pretty occupied for an hour and a half, two hours. Including Mrs Collins, who used to be a district nurse. They live in Buick Street, almost opposite the fire station."

Steven remembered that accident, right in front of the Centennial Memorial at the beach end of Buick Street.

"And the burglary?"

"Collins was lucky there. Chap nearly didn't bother going back to the shop. Then realized everything had happened so fast maybe he hadn't locked up. First thing he spotted was the watches gone from the window. Unlocked the door, went inside, found the others gone."

"One and a half hours, eh? Someone was moving pretty fast. What does Fairbrother think of Collins?"

"Steady. Reliable. Backbone of the force. Did his best to clear him. Could only prove a definite police link."

Steven grimaced. "Well, the pattern's there. And unfortunately Collins is the focal point. What did they do? Double patrols? Set up check points?"

"Usual routine stuff. But——" Peacock spread his hands. "Who can foresee a fire, an accident, or anything else that'd claim police attention. Could patrol for weeks without anything coming

70

up. And a police tie-in meant someone probably knew when the special was in operation."

"Wait a minute. There had to be fires when other men were on nights!"

"There were. But no burglaries. That only seemed to happen when Collins was on duty."

"Maybe that's it. An accomplice making sure Collins had an out!"

Peacock snorted. "Could think of better alibis. And why stick to Collins' night-duty times. Same set-up could operate whoever was on nights. Collins would know he'd need an alibi whenever there was a fire and so forth, on duty, off duty."

"Maybe someone wanted police to think Collins was involved?"

"Only too obvious. And it worked. Pattern couldn't be ignored entirely. Besides, there were other things. For instance, Collins was in the jeweller's shop that day. Took his wife's watch in to be fixed. Shop-owner showed him the digitals."

Steven nodded. "But nothing's happened these last four months. Why the lull? D'you think he's given it away?"

"Like to think so but—fact is, Collins was on suspension six weeks. Kept off nights when reinstated."

"Collins wouldn't like that."

"He didn't. Fairbrother says he kept pestering to be allowed nights. In the end, let him have a burl a couple of weeks ago. Nothing happened. No fires. No accidents. No burglaries."

"Which doesn't prove a thing either way."

"No. Doesn't prove a thing. Could be the inquiry did frighten him off but somehow . . ." He paused, fingering his chin. "Suppose Collins found out Blaney was investigating again? Could that be——No, not a good enough reason. Unless Blaney stumbled on to something else we don't know about."

"Anyway, we can't make him Johnny on the spot," commented Steven. "We know exactly where he was when Blaney was killed. Near me all the time. He's got a perfect out!"

"He always has," said Peacock sourly. "And get this. Collins wasn't supposed to be working to-day. Starts night duty to-morrow so to-day he's free. Fairbrother says he offered to come back, help out. Maybe he had a reason. Didn't have to be you, y'know. He could've stuck close to anyone on duty. Same effect. Problem is, can we prove he needed a story for that time?"

But Steven's mind was going off on another tack. He disagreed with Peacock on one point. Collins had been singularly lucky with his proven alibis. If those two shopkeepers had not revisited their shops when they did, the time element would not have been so conclusive. Without their evidence, Collins would never have succeeded in convincing the tribunal.

Even so, reinstatement, more especially the return to night duty, was a calculated risk. If the same pattern recurred, Collins would face certain dismissal. Reluctantly, perhaps, if police were still convinced of his innocence but a necessary gesture to a public which deserved better protection than could be supplied by a man who attracted burglaries the way Collins did.

CHAPTER VIII

"SHE'S JENNY WHITE," said Kylie when Steven told her about the gaunt woman hovering in the background during their interview with the professor.

"Jenny White?" repeated Steven vaguely.

"Yes. You know. Aunt Florrie's picture."

"Surely not! She does paint. At least, they said so. But like that! She's just a shell. Almost unalive."

Kylie shrugged. "Maybe that's it. Her emotions are so restrained caring for Tommy, she compensates by pouring her feelings on canvas. Dig? Anyway, Aunt Florrie says she lives in Petone."

Aunt Florrie's picture! thought Steven. He could still recall that first moment of impact. For the first time trite phrases took on meaning. Use of true colour. Mixture of realism and symbolism. Strength and texture. Strength from Mrs White!

"Death by the River"—a tranquil scene, sunlit-blue water lapping grey stones. Against this cool background glowed a greenstone mere, slanted towards the edge of the painting—and the hand, the dead hand of the warrior who had died by the river.

That hand! It dominated the canvas, intruded, flaunting its message: that life was not all tranquillity, life was death.

Steven recalled all this as he stood in front of Mrs White on Saturday morning. He tried to see past the brittle façade, failed. She was simply Mrs White, fragile, withdrawn.

Tommy was not at home, she explained. He was fishing on Petone wharf with Judd Cumming, a retired civil servant, who often took Tommy fishing, exploring around the valley.

Steven protested that Tommy should have been kept home, in case the police needed to talk with him again.

Mrs White stiffened, a sharp note creeping into her tired voice. Tommy was perfectly safe with Mr Cumming who offered to keep him occupied. It had been her practice to see that Tommy was out of doors as much as possible so she had no intention of altering things now, police or no police.

At that pointed reminder of Tommy's failing health, Steven had to agree that keeping him in on such a fine day would serve no purpose, hoped she did not mind if he also went down to the wharf.

He thought about Mrs White while driving along the Esplanade, idly noting the people on the beach, sprawling on the sands, swimming. Yachts dotted the harbour with bright sails. Here and there a power boat churned the water into foam. In front of the rowing club, an eight was readying a shell for a practice run.

Like a Jenny White canvas, thought Steven. Tranquil, placid, the police car a focal point hinting at hidden tensions. Somehow it did not gel. The police car was too ordinary. Something more shocking was needed, something utterly incongruous. Like a dead policeman in fancydress.

Steven stopped the car, climbed out, strolled on to the wharf. He found his quarry easily enough, halfway along. Tommy in plaid shirt, faded jeans, playing his hand line; Judd Cumming in comfortable grey slacks, blue shirt, cutting up bait.

He paused beside them, taking in the scene, men and boys at the far end intent on their lines, sufficiently remote to ensure complete privacy. He squatted down beside Cumming.

"How's the fishing?" he asked quietly.

Cumming looked at him sideways. "Couple of spotties, that's all. Deep sea spotties. Tommy got them both."

He baited the hook with cut-up herring, threw the line into the sea. Tommy did not look up, sat watching his line, working it gently every now and then.

Steven showed his identification to Cumming, moved closer. "I've come to see Tommy actually."

Cumming shook his head. "Waste of time while he's fishing. What d'you want to know?"

"One or two things," said Steven cautiously.

Cumming snorted. "About this policeman business, is it? Tommy doesn't know a thing. Someone's trying to use him. Plain as the nose on your face. Even a dumb cop could see that."

"That is one line of inquiry, Mr Cumming. Even so, Tommy is our only link. It's virtually necessary to get through, find out the something he knows that might lead us elsewhere."

Cumming eyed him sardonically. "Sounds like you're getting nowhere fast. But if it'll help clear Tommy . . ." He chewed his underlip, looked thoughtful. "Tell you what. I'll do the questioning. Got a system. What particular thing did you want to know?"

Steven hesitated. He did not want to bring this garrulous old man into orbit, yet using him could produce results.

"All right. We want to know about a key. We also want to know exactly how he knew where to be at the right time."

Tommy caught a fish at that moment, landed the flopping particle of life on the wooden planking. Cumming quietly took over, disengaged the hook, spread the wings of the gurnard to show Tommy the butterfly markings.

"That's a good one, lad. Sweet flesh." He placed the fish beside the two spotties. "Quite a panful, eh? Now, give me your line."

Tommy hardly glanced at Steven, probably not even recognizing him. He sat beside Cumming, waiting patiently while the old man rebaited his hook, extremely slowly.

Cumming started to speak in a soft monotone, monosyllabic, soothing. Presently, Tommy joined in, using the same pitch, the same rambling chatter, an almost perfect imitation.

"Yes, that's right, me boy. More bait. More fish. Your ma will be pleased, won't she, lad? Right pleased with her boy, Tommy. My Tommy can run. My Tommy can fish. My Tommy can turn a key in a lock, in a door, in a lock."

"No lock. No door. Bury key. Pretty flowers."

Cumming looked at Steven who nodded briefly. "Key in flowers. Key on ground. Key in door. Key on path."

"Key," Tommy repeated doubtfully. "Key. Red stone. Red stone. White stone. Gun. Red stone. Key. Pretty flowers."

75

Steven started when Tommy said gun. Gun and key meant red stone, white stone to Tommy and pretty flowers. The marigolds. And the Gregg's patio was paved with large concrete blocks, red and white alternately.

"Key. Gun. Red stone," went on Cumming. "And a bad man. Bad man come. You wait. You know. You wait."

"I wait. They told me. The whispers. The wind. Mummy said. Dreamtime. They told me. Wait. Bad man. Bad man. Bang, you're dead."

The rebaiting was finished. Cumming handed the line to Tommy who immediately returned to his possy by the shed, threw it into the sea.

"Any use to you?" asked Cumming.

"Some," agreed Steven. "D'you do that often? Tommy played up pretty readily. As though he's used to it."

Cumming rubbed his hands on a piece of crumpled newspaper; pulled out a pipe with tobacco already tamped down, lit it.

"Yes. A bit. Y'see Tommy says something, skitters off on to something else. If I want to know what he's getting at, keeps him pinned down."

"So, if I wanted Tommy to go to a certain place at a specific time—well, what do I do?"

"Tell him immediately before the time specified."

"Couldn't I tell him a few days before? The day before?"

"We—ell, you could prime him up a bit. Tell him over and over. Get the idea into his head. But you'd still have to remind him. No concentration, y'see."

"He's concentrating well enough now," laughed Steven.

"Yes, this is right up his alley. He'll sit for hours fishing. No fidgeting and jumping around like most."

He looked towards the end of the wharf where two boys were squabbling over a tangled line. The man with them spoke sharply and they settled down again.

"I noticed you baited the hook," commented Steven.

"Always do. Never let Tommy play with knives or anything sharp. That's one of the rules."

"His father lets him play with guns."

76

"Not likely to cut himself on a gun." Cumming paused to suck a few minutes on his pipe. "Y'see Tommy's not properly balanced, co-ordinated. Now and then he loses functional concentration. If he had a knife in his hand at those times, he'd carve himself up."

Which proved once again that it was not Tommy who climbed on to Mrs Gregg's bench, took careful aim through the open window.

"Can I have your address, Mr Cumming? Someone will be coming around for a statement later." When the old man stiffened, he added hastily, "Routine. Everyone connected makes a statement."

Cumming supplied the address, lapsed into silence, puffing contentedly at his pipe. Steven sat beside him, letting the sun soak in, listening to the waves slurping against the wharf.

In the corner of the harbour by the Hutt Road, skiers were tuning their boats. Steven watched the first few runs with interest, smiled when a skier tumbled, had to be retrieved from the water.

He turned, looked back over the two-mile beach. More pleasure boats were being trundled seaward. Sea Scouts made a smart picture exercising in front of their "ship".

It was so pleasant, he felt he could spend the day there until he caught sight of a traffic officer on a motor cycle passing the Centennial Memorial. Lance Brendon, maybe.

Steven looked at his watch guiltily, clambered quickly to his feet. "I'll have to be going now," he said to Cumming, who nodded absently, eyes focused on the lazy sea.

As he hurried along, Steven watched the traffic officer coming closer, nodded to himself when the man swung towards the wharf gates, stopped by the police car, looked around.

Brendon had dismounted, was removing helmet and gauntlets when Steven reached him. He flicked his gloves in a derisive salute.

"Thought it might be you. Someone I knew anyway."

He looked smart, efficient, in brown breeches, white silk shirt crisp fair hair gleaming in the sun.

Steven grinned. "See you're a cowboy again. Like the bike?"

"So—so. How long d'you want my car anyway?"

"Couple of days. Depends on what the lab chaps find."

"You think they'll find something?"

"Something. Mightn't tie in with this case but it could be interesting." His lips twitched slightly. "Wanted to see you about something else, though."

"Oh," said Brendon and Steven noticed the wary look.

"This secret project Blaney was on. D'you know anything about it?"

Brendon's face went blank. "What secret project?"

"The little black book, remember? The one you tried to swipe right under our noses. Took a hell of a risk, didn't you?"

The traffic officer smiled bleakly. "Maybe. Wasn't for everyone to see. When they told me Joe'd copped it, I thought of those law boys swarming all over. One of them got his hands on it, wouldn't take long to put two and two together, make five."

"How far had Blaney got, d'you know?"

"As far as need be without absolute proof. Fairbrother said nothing doing without concrete evidence. And that's exactly what he didn't have. We were waiting for the next break."

"The next break?"

"Yeh. Collins needs to be on nights again. We figured next week. Monday, Tuesday, Wednesday maybe. After that, well, we wait again."

"Collins starts night shift to-night."

"That's right."

"So, why not to-night? To-morrow?"

Brendon shrugged, shook his head. Steven felt a wave of irritation. Obviously Blaney had uncovered the catalyst, the one ingredient that triggered the burglaries. And Brendon was playing it smart, not talking.

"How d'you fit in? He wasn't supposed to discuss it with outsiders."

"He discussed it with me," said Brendon mildly. "I'm not law. I'm traffic. But we do work with police, y'know. So I'm not exactly an outsider. Joe started talking about Mr X but I'd

78

heard the chatter. Told him not to fiddle. If he wanted to use me, use me. Don't play games. After that," he slapped his gauntlets against his shining boots. "After that, well, we got together, tore into it. Think we've got something now."

"Exactly what?"

"I said 'we'. Now, it's only me. And that's the way it stays until I'm good and ready to tell everybody Joe's idea."

"We could go to your superiors. Demand your co-operation."

Brendon flared suddenly. "You do just that. See how far it gets you. Like I said, we, the department, co-operate with police. But that means a formal request, buster. You ask nice and polite and maybe we'll dish out."

"You'll dish out!" snapped Steven.

"Yeh? When I'm good and ready. Like, maybe next week. Nothing happens then, out of my hands. Fairbrother can have the whole caboodle. But right now I'm going Joe's way. Guess we owe him that much. And he wasn't aiming to tell police anything! Not till we had it right on the line."

Their heated exchange was interrupted by the sound of brakes, scream of rubber. They spun to see a small red car stopped by the kerb.

"Oh! Oh!" said Brendon. "Trouble!"

Arline Muir opened the door, stepped out. She looked angry. She stalked around the car, across the pavement, planted herself belligerently in front of the traffic officer.

Tight-eyed, tight-lipped, she barely glanced at Steven, her whole attention clawing at Brendon like a tiger on a leash.

"I've been looking for you—you murderer!" She hissed. "You killed him, didn't you? Didn't you? You nearly killed him once before. This time you made sure. Didn't you!"

The words tumbled out, pent-up emotions making her body tremble. Brendon's eyes flicked in Steven's direction, he stepped forward, began to shake the girl, shake her, shake her.

"Hey! Hey! Stop that, Arline. You don't know what you're saying. Stop it! You're making a fool of yourself!"

The girl twisted free, lunged at Steven. "Listen to me. You've got to listen to me. He's hated Joe ever since—ever since I dropped him. Because I preferred Joe. Ask him! Ask him!"

79

Steven looked over her head at Brendon who shrugged. "Sure I bloodied his nose. Wouldn't you? Must've been nuts! He was doing me a favour!"

The studied insult brought a dull flush to the girl's cheeks. She gasped as though struck. Steven intervened hastily. "Joe Blaney was shot, Miss Muir. There's a difference, y'know. Quite a difference, between punching a fellow on the nose and shooting him."

"But he had a gun!" she flung back. "A hand gun with a swept-back handle. I saw it. Last Sunday. He came back to the flat. Dumped his coat on the chair and I heard this—this thunk. I wondered. Had a look."

"You're sure? Quite sure?"

"I'm sure!" Quiet now, anger spent, she turned, walked slowly to the car, climbed aboard, not looking back. Steven thought she was crying as she drove away, crying at last.

He faced Brendon again. The transport man finished donning his helmet, stared defiantly back.

"Did you have a gun?" Steven asked.

"No. She's making that up out of the whole cloth. Maybe she really believes——" He shook his head, pulled his motorcycle round, kicked it into life. "Anyway, if you want to arrest me, you know where to find me."

He waited astride the motorcycle, lips curled. When Steven made no move, he swung out on to the road.

As he sped off in the same direction as Arline, he called, "Seen this morning's paper yet?"

Steven felt cold. He climbed into the police car, picked up the paper from the front seat.

A four inch photograph of Arline Muir smiled at him under the headline "Slain Policeman's Fiancée Would-Be Model." The fillout was devoted to Arline's ambition to model, her measurements, hobbies. Blaney's death was mentioned—in a black edged block asking for information on the Luger.

Steven flung the paper away in disgust. He understood what Brendon meant by his parting remark. A girl who lent herself to such publicity would do anything to attract attention. Anything!

80

Peacock seemed to be of the same opinion. "Certainly recovered quickly enough after we left."

"The magic word 'reporter' no doubt," said Steven drily. "Just unfortunate there was no world-shattering news for the front page. Otherwise it would've been decently interred in the women's pages as usual."

Jonas was more interested in the interview with Tommy, questioning him closely. "Well, yes. As you say, it could be the patio. But don't forget the drive is surfaced with brick chips. Take your pick. Now, that bit about having to tell Tommy immediately before. Notice Collins talking to him at all?"

"He said something to Tommy as he went past, yes. When I first met them. Y'know, couple of words. Not much."

"But enough, eh?" said Peacock. "Cumming stopped rather abruptly, didn't he?"

"He'd finished baiting the hook. Couldn't drag it out any longer."

"Perhaps. Or maybe the mention of Tommy's mother. Didn't expect that, I'll bet. Thought he'd bring out routine stuff. Instead—the whispers, the wind, Mummy said, dreamtime. What exactly did Mummy say? The whispers were just the wind? He was dreaming?"

"More important, when did she say it? Chronological order wouldn't mean anything to Tommy. Could've happened when she was trying to find out who 'they' were."

"Could be. Y'know, Mrs White kept awful quiet at that interview. Awful quiet."

Steven looked at him sharply. Maybe Jonas had something there. Maybe those tired eyes concealed more than the lively mind of Jenny White.

"If only we could trace the gun!" he said impatiently.

Peacock's head jerked up. "Yes, of course. You were out. We've got a lead there, at least. But grab yourself something to eat. We'll be interviewing the owner at one-fifteen."

CHAPTER IX

"GREGG SEEMS TO have cleared himself," said Steven, turning the typed pages. "Thought there'd be a woman involved but I'd never guess the reason. Not in a hundred years. You'd think he'd have more common, to use his own expression."

Peacock grunted. "Wouldn't be the first man to get the jitters when his insides start playing up. Do anything but go to a doctor, that type. Gregg just thought he'd try this Mrs Pennell. See if the laying on of hands could shift the ulcer or whatever."

Constable Bruce Wilkins knocked on the door, entered, a sheaf of papers in his hand. "Keith Hounsell's here, sir," he said, placing the papers in front of Peacock.

"Right. But before—shut the door, will you?" When Wilkins complied, he continued. "He's positively identified the gun?"

"Yes, sir. It's his all right."

"I see. You're a friend of Hounsell's, I understand."

"Yes, sir."

"And you didn't know anything about this Luger?"

"No, sir. He'd have been a fool to tell me."

"And you'd be a fool to admit it, eh?" The hard eyes bored into the uniform man's face but Wilkins made no comment, stared stonily back.

"So! Well, we're ready for Hounsell. Bring him in."

Wilkins nodded, retreated for a moment to return with Keith Hounsell, the owner of the gun.

Sandy, weathered, left cheek puckered by a thread of scar, he took the chair offered, waited quietly for Peacock to speak.

After the preliminary questions, Peacock leaned back, stared thoughtfully at Hounsell, who used the pause to pull out a cigarette, tap it, light it. Peacock frowned, not at Hounsell's action, but because his own long stare had had no effect. Hounsell sat completely relaxed, waiting.

"When did you arrive back, Mr Hounsell?" Peacock asked.

"Ten-twenty-five. Stayed overnight at Palmerston North. Drove down this morning."

"You stayed overnight in Palmerston? My information is that you left here Tuesday morning."

"I did. Drove to Palmerston. Went to Auckland by plane. Came back yesterday. To Palmerston, that is. Meant to stay the weekend but saw the bit in the paper about Joe."

"Why didn't you fly to Auckland direct, Mr Hounsell?"

Hounsell dragged slowly on his cigarette. "My father lives in Palmerston. Went to pick him up."

"There was a reason, I take it. Business or pleasure?"

"Business."

Peacock waited but no further explanation was offered. Steven suppressed a smile. This one was going to be difficult. Each item of information would have to be coaxed out with the precise question.

"All right," said Peacock sharply. "Tell us about it."

Hounsell nodded. "Yeh, I suppose that's necessary. My father's a lawyer. Retired. I needed his advice on this—business deal. That's why he went along."

"This business deal," prompted Peacock.

Hounsell regarded him coolly. "You must've read about it in the papers. I'm one of the treasure seekers."

Steven sat up, looked at Hounsell with new interest.

"The *Elingamite*," he breathed, remembering the newspaper article on the ship wrecked off Three Kings Islands in 1902.

Hounsell's eyes glinted. "Yes, the *Elingamite*. We brought up 80-pounds weight of silver when we located her. Loose stuff lying around. This year we're going at it more scientifically. Proper expedition. Supposed to be $34,000 in silver coins on board when she went down. That's why I dragged the old man in. Been researching the legal aspects. Make sure we don't lose by it."

"Fixed it all up, have you?" Peacock asked genially.

"Yeh. Fixed it all up."

"So yesterday you were in Palmerston. All day?"

"Most of it. Arrived early morning. Went up to the house, mucked around a bit. Then went for a wander around the old home town."

"Where exactly?"

"Oh, around. Looked at a couple of the new areas, ended up by the river, Esplanade, Massey, that direction."

"Alone?"

Again the look of faint surprise. "Yeh. Alone. Why not?"

"Did you meet anyone you knew? Could vouch for you?"

"Ten years since I've been home. Don't know anyone much. Went to Massey College mainly to see my brother but he was in classes. Hung around till five. Had a chinwag."

"Exactly what time did you leave the house to explore?"

"Oh, around eleven or thereabouts."

"You stopped somewhere for lunch then?"

"Nope. Don't eat by the clock. Filled up before I went. Didn't eat again till I got back. Around six."

Steven eyed Hounsell speculatively. For six hours he had been driving around Palmerston North alone. Allegedly. In that time he could have driven down and back easily. Flown down and back. Plane times would need to be checked but it could be done.

"All right," said Peacock. "You arrived at your lodging place, Hudson House, at ten-twenty-five. And then?"

"Had a natter with Siggy, Mr Sigley, the owner. About the Three Kings bit—Joe. Went along to my room, opened the door. Could see straight off someone'd been messing around. Locked the door again. Called Bruce. Bruce Wilkins."

"Did you know then the Luger had gone?"

"Guessed. Had it locked away, top left-hand drawer. Drawer busted, forced. Not surprised. Half expected it. Saw your box in the paper, y'see. And Siggy filled me in. About Joe, the Luger, Tommy White. Too much of a coincidence, I mean. An unregistered hand gun wanted. And mine gone. Had to be mine."

"Anything else missing?"

"Yeh. Small things. Pocket transistor. Depth gauge. Compass. Small things."

84

Small things, thought Steven. Things a man could put in his pocket, not be noticed.

"Yet the room had been thoroughly searched, they say. Looking for anything in particular, d'you think?"

"Looking for the Luger," said Hounsell positively. "Didn't want just a gun. Three rifles on the wall, y'know. Easy to get at. No, it was the Luger he wanted."

"Was it generally known you had it?"

"Nobody heard about it from me, Inspector."

"Nobody! You're cobbers with Wilkins, aren't you? Blaney?"

"Not a thing I'd talk to police about. Put them on a spot."

"What about Brendon? He isn't police."

Hounsell gave a sour smile. "Tell Lance anything, you've told Joe. Doesn't know how to keep his trap shut, that fellow."

"So it boils down to this. Nobody knew about the gun yet someone searched the room for it. Contradiction there, Mr Hounsell."

"Correction, Inspector. I said it wasn't generally known. I said certain people didn't know. But I didn't say nobody knew. Someone definitely knew about it all right."

"Why? Because it was stolen?"

Hounsell shook his head. "No. Someone entered my room before. Found the Luger then. That's why I locked it away. Fitted a special lock."

"When was this?"

"A month ago. 15 October, I think. I could check. Came off work early. Feeling woozy. Went to the drawer to get some Disprins. That's where I kept the Luger before. Spotted straight off someone had been at it."

"Did you report it?"

"You kidding? Couldn't even prove it to anyone else. Just the way things were, well, disarranged. Besides I'd have looked a bit of a dill reporting something like that to the police."

"Did you have any idea who it might be? Someone at Hudson House?"

Hounsell shrugged. "Thought so at the time. Laid a few traps but none of them sprung. Anyway, mightn't be any connection. They reckon this is an outside job."

He leaned forwards, mashed his cigarette into the empty ashtray. Peacock looked thoughtful. "Mr Hounsell," he said at last, "why did you tell us about the Luger?"

Hounsell looked puzzled. "It was stolen."

"That's right. But no one knew you had it, least of all police. You could've reported the burglary. Left it at that. Not mentioned the gun. As it is, you've volunteered yourself into a prosecution for illegal possession."

"So!" Hounsell's eyes mocked the inspector. "You've got the gun. You'd have traced it back to me eventually. Take time, but you've got the means. How'd it look then, Inspector? When you found I hadn't reported it? Besides, the sooner you knew——"

Peacock nodded. "Yes. As you say, Mr Hounsell. Time is important. Thanks for coming forward. It's possible we will be getting in touch with you later."

Hounsell stood up. "Do that! Joe was—he was one of the best. And it was my gun, dammit."

He grimaced, swung on his heel, left the room quickly, pulling the door sharply behind him.

"Seemed upset," said Steven quietly.

"And hated like hell showing it. Anyway that lets Brendon off the hook. He may have had a gun but not that particular one. Still there Tuesday. Get Wilkins in, will you?"

Steven went to the door, looked out. Bruce Wilkins was talking to Hounsell. Steven beckoned. The young constable patted his friend on the shoulder, hurried over to Steven.

"One or two things," said Peacock blandly. "Did Hounsell report the burglary to police or to you personally."

"To me, sir. Asked for me. Told me his room had been done over, wanted to know the usual procedure. I offered to report it, make it official, in case something worthwhile had been taken. He said he knew something worthwhile was missing. Told me about the Luger. Said he was scared it might be the one that killed Joe Blaney. And it is, of course."

"Good. How far have we got so far?"

"Forensic's at Hudson House, now, sir. We've interviewed eight men, including the owner, Ed Sigley. That leaves seven. Two playing cricket, one's skin-diving, one's gone home for the weekend and three are sleeping. They work nights. Over at Stacey's. Getting up around two-thirty to three."

"All right. Tell me about Hudson House. Decent place?"

"Fairly good, sir. Used to be full board but Mrs Sigley died last year so Sigley turned it into bed-and-breakfast. Caters for process workers, such like."

"Single rooms?"

"Now it is. Two storey weatherboard. Old type. High stud. Big renovation job a few years back. Ripped out most of the inside. Rebuilt for more accommodation. Rooms smaller but plenty of space for one man."

"And accommodates fifteen?"

"Yes, sir. That's about the limit. Some of the downstair rooms still the original size, lounge, dining-room. And there's a three-bedroom unit at the back."

Peacock nodded. "We'll need to go over there shortly but first—how long have you known Hounsell?"

"Went to high school with him. Palmerston North Boys'."

"He said his father's a lawyer. He has a brother at Massey College. Yet he's a fitter's mate."

"Keith's odd man out. His brother at Massey is Professor Connelly Hounsell. Another brother's taken over his father's partnership. And his sister's matron at Middlemore Hospital."

"He'd be a good deal younger then?"

"A good fifteen years. Couldn't stand the academic life. Cleared out before he was twenty. Worked his way around the world pretty near. Came back about five years ago. Tried different jobs, finally settled for deer culling. But last year he contracted pneumonia. Had to be carried out. Doctor told him to give it a rest."

"Police record?"

"Some. Disturbing the peace. Resisting arrest. That kind of thing. Nothing recent. A bit hotheaded."

"Where'd he get that scar? In a brawl?"

"No, sir. A case of the deer getting a bit of their own back, he always says. A cast antler caught in a bush and he had to barge right into it. Halfway through shooting out a block so his

87

mate patched him up and he carried on. That's why it healed that way."

"D'you go to Hudson House very much?"

"Quite a bit. Play cards. Yarn. Siggy turns it on for us. Timid type. Gets a kick out of associating with the doers."

"Did you ever talk about the Ponderosa set-up while there?"

For the first time Wilkins looked uncomfortable. "Yes, sir. When it was first mooted. Tossed it around a bit. Keith offered to lend Joe a rifle but I checked and it wasn't required."

"D'you remember who was there when this happened?"

"Well, yes. Sigley, Keith, and one of the night-shift chaps, I think. Puku Thompson."

"Tell me, Constable, exactly how many men at Hudson House knew Blaney was going to be a bandit?"

Wilkins hesitated. "I don't know, sir. After all, we didn't swear anyone to secrecy or anything."

Steven remembered how casually Collins had told him about Blaney. Probably everyone on the force thought it was a big laugh.

Peacock sighed, looked at Steven. "All right. We'd better get over to Hudson House. See what's what."

Wilkins coughed. "May I suggest going out the back, sir. Through the rec. Quite a bit shorter."

Behind the court house, they manoeuvred through children's swings and slides till they reached the bitumen path around the main playing area. Two games of cricket were in progress, languid in the afternoon sun. In front of the grandstand, a blond man was teaching youngsters the rudiments of a good starting position.

On the eastern boundary, the new block of the technical institute overshadowed the brick-and-glass structure of the original college. They traversed a narrow alley between the two buildings, turned right at a galvanized fence behind the engineering section, stopped by a gate crudely fashioned from a single sheet of iron.

Wilkins opened the gate. They entered the small neat yard of Hudson House. A few shrubs grew tiredly against the unpainted fence, the three-bedroom unit with workshop attached.

Ed Sigley came to the door as they approached, slight, ordinary, features as indefinite as a child's drawing, face a circle, mouth a line, eyes dots, a scribble of grey hair. Steven looked into the workshop, was surprised to see massive wood carvings in traditional design.

Wilkins introduced Sigley to Peacock who asked genially, "Are the night-shift men up yet, d'you know?"

"Should be. Called them an hour ago. Told them you'd be coming over to question them."

"Don't you get their breakfast for them?"

Sigley shrugged. "No. Leave the stuff out. They get it themselves. Besides Charlie's a better cook than I am."

He kept caressing the tool in his hand, anxious to return to his hobby. Peacock dismissed him with a nod and Sigley scurried back to his interrupted work.

"Charlie?" Peacock asked Wilkins.

"Charlie Heath," said Wilkins. "Used to work in a restaurant. The fat one's Puku Thompson, the skinny one's Alan Bristowe."

They entered the large kitchen streamlined to the enth degree. Every labour-saving device seemed to be in its place.

The three shift men were busy; Heath dishing out eggs and bacon, craggy face intent; Thompson buttering toast, full lips pursed; Bristowe pouring water into a teapot, gangling, twenty years younger than the other two.

Peacock and Wilkins went through to Hounsell's room, Steven paused to introduce himself. "We're here for this Blaney business, y'know, so we'll be wanting statements from you all. Particularly what you were doing yesterday afternoon."

"Why us?" growled Thompson.

"Everyone at Hudson House, Mr Thompson. Routine. You'd be surprised how many statements we take simply to prove what didn't happen."

"The process of elimination, eh?" smiled Heath. "But I don't think we can tell you anything much. We all went up town to see the show."

"Together?"

"Why no. Puku went earliest. To the pub, eh, Puku? Sonny here was on the telephone when I left. 'Phoning your mum, weren't you, Sonny? Me? I was on Jackson Street about the

89

same time you met up with Harvey Collins. Maybe Harvey even saw me."

Steven nodded. "Well, that's the kind of thing we want. An outline of your movements with at least one corroborating witness." He turned to go, paused in the doorway. "By the way, d'you always get up at this time?"

"Saturdays," Thompson said through a mouthful of toast. "Weekends we sleep nights so Monday just an afternoon kip. Rest of the week we sleep till four. At least usually. Yesterday, of course, we were up at twelve. Y'know, Ponderosa Day."

"I know," smiled Steven. He left them to their meal, stepped into the long passage dissecting the house.

A young constable guarded the room on the south side where Peacock was examining the splintered drawer of a lowboy, Wilkins and Hounsell standing superfluously by. Forensic had finished their work, taken away their samples, pieces of evidence. Even so the room seemed crowded.

Steven moved to the window, studied the tell-tale marks on the sill. He leaned out, looked right and left.

The house next door seemed close, built, as was Hudson House, the regulation distance from the boundary. The narrow gap to the wooden fence was used as a minor storage area, lengths of wood, plastic containers lying on the ground, a plank gate separating it from the yard.

At the street end, a large camelia flourished, glossy green leaves festooned with white japonica blooms. Anyone working at this window would have been effectively screened from observation except from the next-door house.

Steven looked reflectively at the creeper-covered wall opposite, at the upper bedroom windows.

He turned to Hounsell. "D'you know who lives next door?"

Hounsell took a step forward. "Yes. Professor White. And that window up there, that's Tommy's bedroom."

CHAPTER X

"BACK TO SQUARE one," said Peacock. He turned away from the window, stood legs apart, rocked back and forth on the soles of his feet.

Steven found himself examining the room minutely, divan bed, built-in furniture, three guns racked on the wall, a Parker Hale .30-06, a P14 .303, a Winchester .207. He moved closer to the gun-wall, disgusted with himself for not realizing earlier the Whites lived so close.

"That creeper," said Peacock. "A bit worn in places."

"Tommy's mountain," said Hounsell, lapsed into silence.

Wilkins explained. "Tommy climbs up and down there, sir. Not just creeper. Steel rungs here and there, where the creeper thins out. Doc White put them in to make it safer."

"You've seen Tommy do this?"

"Yes, sir. Quite an education. It's not just a ladder to him. Pretends it's a rock face or similar, searches for handholds, foot-holds. Almost think he was using crampons."

Peacock swung back to the window, measuring distances from house to fence, from fence to broached window. "Wouldn't take too much effort to get over here," he growled. He joined Steven, gazing at the dull sheen of gun barrels, the gleam of walnut stocks.

"These guns, Mr Hounsell. D'you clean them in this room?"

"Have done."

"By the window?"

"Naturally."

"Tommy would be able to see you from his bedroom window?"

"Could be."

"And the Luger?"

"No, sir. Only time I ever had that out, night time. Blinds down. Couldn't take the risk of being overlooked."

Peacock returned to the window, pulled the shade. A heavy holland blind, plain, boarding-house for the use of, blocking all outside view. He let the blind go, to roll back into its usual position.

"So Tommy didn't know you had the Luger?"

"Couldn't swear to that, Inspector. Someone knew."

"But you thought someone in Hudson House?"

"I did. But I didn't check for breaking and entering."

Peacock played the question-and-answer game for a while longer, gave up, beckoned to Steven, Wilkins, left Hounsell to his own musings. The only person in the kitchen when they went through was Alan Bristowe, dreamily stacking the dishwasher.

Next door, Peacock knocked twice, peered into several windows, before deciding the Whites were not at home. He went through the hedged area at the back to the fence, nodding when he found a gate similar to the one at Hudson House.

He opened it, stepped into the alley which ended a few feet beyond, stared thoughtfully from galvanized iron to the brick and glass of the engineering block, shrugged, led the way out of the cul-de-sac.

No one spoke. No one showed the slightest interest in the progress of the cricket games as they walked through the rec.

Grimly Steven settled down to read more reports while Peacock elected to consult Senior Sergeant Fairbrother. The case was dead. He could feel it. Once again they were defeated by the impassable barrier of Tommy White.

Steven had felt this way before but it did not alter procedure. They would go on asking questions, checking, re-checking, seeking the one element that could lead them to a solution.

Which meant he would have to work on his rest day again. It was not unexpected but with nothing developing it seemed arbitrary.

He would have to ring Kylie shortly, tell her their proposed trip to Masterton would have to be postponed. Maybe he would leave it till he went home. He had to go to Masterton for a court case Monday, so maybe she could accompany him. The shop could manage without her for one day and, while he was in court, Kylie could visit her parents.

Steven had planned a final conference on Sunday but now they would have to be content with a hurried consultation immediately before court. Still, that was the way things happened.

There was one thing he promised himself. He would make time to discuss this present case with his father-in-law, Senior Sergeant Nathan Peacock. Jonas would probably suggest it anyway as he had a hearty respect for his older brother's acumen, even if he did outrank him.

Reluctantly he forced himself to concentrate on reports in front of him. They did not tell him much. Most of the residents of Hudson House had been at work on Friday, which meant their elimination from the Blaney case if not from the theft of the Luger.

That left Sigley, Hounsell and the three shift workers for further scrutiny. Sigley had attended Ponderosa Day with friends who were able to support his statement while Hounsell . . . Steven pulled the airport findings to him, read them through again. A plane arrived daily from Palmerston North at 12.45 pm which would give Hounsell ample time to drive to Petone, commit the murder, drive back to catch the return flight at 3.15 pm.

Investigation at the airport car-rental agencies disclosed the weekend hiring of a car by a passenger vaguely resembling Hounsell but the contract said Albert Tunny Leybourne. The Feilding police, checking at the given address, found Leybourne still at home, unaware that his licence was missing.

It looked promising until further probing revealed that the Friday plane had been delayed 55 minutes at take-off so its late arrival meant Hounsell could not possibly have been in Petone until well after two o'clock.

At five the cadet brought in more statements from Hudson House, including those of the shift workers.

"Anything from that rental alert?" Steven asked.

"No, sir. You want to know as soon as we have word?"

93

"Yes. Got nothing to do with this case apparently, but who-ever he is he's hiding something."

He sorted through typed sheets, studying the ones of the shift workers. Each man was able to prove his presence in Jackson Street during the staged hold-up. Collins recalled seeing Heath briefly before speaking to Steven.

Bristowe was late, delayed by a toll call to Hastings but he had seen the battle of The Golden Horseshoe, watching from a shop doorway with two of the girl assistants. He named as witness Charlie Heath who had been in the crowd close by, had helped him and the girls replace the boxes they had used as personal grandstands.

Puku Thompson. Steven smiled at the revelation of Cholmon-deley Everett as Thompson's given names. Puku naturally had a barman as his witness, having spent the afternoon from one on in the bar except when watching the robbery with two drink-ing companions, unnamed.

Peacock came in at quarter to six, sat down, brought out the usual packet of gum, thoughtfully inserted two pellets in his mouth.

Steven, watching the brooding face, decided to wait for Peacock to speak. The inspector replaced his packet of gum, looked directly at Steven with a sour smile.

"We've had it now," he said gruffly. "White refuses to let anyone interrogate Tommy. On medical grounds, he says."

"But why? Tommy's the only one——"

"He thinks Tommy did it." He sighed. "Maybe he's right."

Steven could not tell whether he meant the professor was right in thinking Tommy did it or in refusing to allow any further questioning.

"D'you think it would've made any difference?" he asked.

Peacock looked at him, did not answer. He indicated the half-finished analysis. "Anything there?"

"Nothing much. Everybody cleared for Friday so far pending confirmation of statements."

A discreet knock and the cadet came in to hand a piece of paper to Peacock. He read it, grimaced. "Hounsell's gun was taken before Thursday night. The bruise on the sill contained

94

rain water. Only time it's rained this week was on Thursday at five for one hour."

Steven started. "Thursday! There's something in Sigley's statement. Here it is. Spring-cleaned Hounsell's room Wednesday morning as requested. Thursday morning went shopping. Always does marketing Thursday morning."

"Looks like Thursday morning then."

"Yes. And there's a bit in Thompson's statement. Let me see. Yes. Thompson sleeps directly above Hounsell's room. Says he was awakened Thursday morning by some sharp noise. Listened a while, decided he was dreaming, went back to sleep."

"When the drawer was forced, eh? Any idea of the time?"

Steven shook his head. "No. Says maybe middle of the morning or earlier. Later, he'd never have got back to sleep."

"And Heath? Bristowe? They'd be home."

"Heath, next room to Thompson. Sleeps like a log, he says. Didn't hear a thing. Bristowe's on the other side of the house."

"Wonder what Tommy was doing Thursday morning."

"Mrs White should know. No need to question Tommy."

"Probably wouldn't remember, anyway. Now, you've got this Masterton case on Monday, haven't you? Well, I want you off it. Get hold of Nathan. See if he can arrange something so you're out of it. Can do?"

"Can do. My day off to-morrow. I'd already planned to go up to Masterton, take Kylie to see her folks."

Peacock laughed. "Right. So it's your day off. Take it. Do whatever else you've planned but get off that case. And ring me when you get back. Might have some new instructions for you."

He did not sound hopeful but Steven was too elated to notice. He rang the shop, arranged to pick up Kylie in half an hour.

He was crossing the footpath when a soft voice said, "Hi, copper. How's the case going?"

He turned to face Judy Clark, red mouth smiling, dark eyes mockingly intimate. "Evening, Miss Clark," said Steven absently, pausing only when she stepped in front of him.

"I was hoping to see you like this. Away from the police station, I mean. Could hardly believe my luck." She looked

95

up at him, close enough for him to catch a wave of perfume.

"I'm just picking up my wife," said Steven brusquely, gesturing towards the shop.

Judy chuckled delightedly. "Oh, you don't need to fling your wife at me for protection. I wanted to see you about Arline. You didn't believe what she said about the gun, did you?"

"Who told you about that? Brendon?"

"Well, yes. He asked me to talk to Arline about it. Make her see how silly she's been. But Arline——" she shrugged. "In one of her moods. Might as well talk to a brick wall. Then I saw you. Thought this a good chance. To fix things, I mean."

"You thought you'd straighten me out, eh?"

"Oh, for heaven's sake! I didn't mean that. I just thought——" she bit her lip. "Y'see, Arline's in love with Lance. Always has been. But Lance, well he's a rover, more fun in the chase than in the capture. You know what I mean. And when she sensed Lance was looking over the field again, well, she made a big play for Joe. Y'know, competition. But it didn't work out that way. She ended up engaged to Joe and Lance went off in a huff."

"More than that. He mixed it with Blaney, didn't he?"

"Well, of course. Reflex action. The male animal resenting any poaching on his preserves. But afterwards——"

"Yeh. Everything sweetness and light. Tell me, Miss Clark, if she's so fond of Brendon, why accuse him like that."

"Make him notice her, that's all. Can't you imagine the scene. He dashes after her, persuades her she's wrong. She tearfully agrees. And then the grand reconciliation."

Steven shook his head. "Sorry, Miss Clark, I don't buy it. She really believed it when she was saying it."

"She didn't y'know. She knew she was quite safe. She could fling that accusation around and no one would take any notice. But no one. Because we all know it was an unfortunate accident!"

She turned to leave but Steven put out a detaining hand. "Wait a moment. What d'you mean? You all know it was an accident?"

Judy frowned. "Well, Tommy White did it. It has to be an

accident. Nobody believes——" She stopped abruptly, suddenly aware of the expression on his face.

"Joe Blaney was murdered," Steven grated. "Tommy White's just a red herring. Someone put that gun in Tommy's hand. After he shot Blaney. D'you understand, you little fool! Joe Blaney was murdered. And Lance Brendon's a prime suspect. Now, go home and tell that to your silly friend."

Immediately Steven was sorry for his outburst. All colour drained from Judy's face. Her fingers fluttered against slack lips.

"No. No. Not Lance! You couldn't believe Lance—"

"We could, you know. We don't go by appearances, Miss Clark. We look for motive, opportunity. Brendon had opportunity. He had a motive of sorts. He may not be top of the charts, but he's certainly in the top ten."

Judy stared at him, silent, incredulous. With a faint moan, she jerked herself free, ran down the deserted street.

"A bit rough on her, weren't you?" said a soft voice behind him. Steven turned to find Kylie closing and locking the shop door. He shrugged.

"Maybe I'm tired," he said. "But she got my goat. Did you hear the cock-and-bull yarn she tried to pull?"

Kylie smiled serenely. "A bit beyond male comprehension, I'll admit. But very female. Especially with the likes of your Arline Muir. She's the type who'd dramatize herself into centre stage, no matter what. And there's nothing more dramatic than a murder inquiry."

CHAPTER XI

"LIKED THAT STRAWBERRY stuff your mother dished up," said Steven on their homeward journey.

"Thought you did," said Kylie. "So I've got the recipe. And Mum said she'll give us some runners. They're not much trouble and it'll be nicer to have our own strawberry patch."

Steven laughed. "So that's what you two were plotting. All right. What about that bit beyond the peach tree. Sheltered but sunny."

Kylie snuggled up against him in agreement. Steven felt good. The day had gone well. He had made his arrangements about the case in the morning so was able to spend the whole afternoon with the family, even though he tended to talk shop with Kylie's father.

He felt relaxed with Nathan Peacock, reaching a degree of comradeship that seemed impossible with Jonas, maybe because he worked in such close contact with the younger brother. Jonas was single-minded in many ways, almost old fashioned. His work was the most important thing in his life, the only thing, and he expected everyone to give it the same devotion he did.

"I'll drop you at home then go round to see Jonas," said Steven. "Maybe something's happened while I was away."

He did not believe that. If there had been any new developments he would have been recalled immediately, but immediately.

They had definitely chosen the right time to return home, little traffic, the Rimutaka Road practically deserted. They passed two cars on the ascent, three parked outside the Summit Restaurant and, now, the home side of the hill wound emptily before them.

Until they reached the lower slopes of the Kaitoke Hills. Steven pulled the car over to the wrong side of the road, braked to a standstill.

"What's wrong?" demanded Kylie, sitting up straight.

"Trouble," he said, starting the car into motion again.

The first sighting of a traffic officer talking to three youths beside a weirdly-painted jalopy had roused only passing interest, but as Steven rounded the next curve the situation had changed.

When he had braked to look down on to the flat, the struggling officer was being held by two of the youths while a third was taking a punch at him with obvious relish.

"That's a traffic officer down there," exclaimed Kylie.

"Yes. Keep an eye on things, will you? I've got to get down there fast." He eased into the next corner, zoomed round the curve so that again the scene below was in view.

"They've got him down on the ground now," said Kylie tightly. "No, he's on his feet again. Taking them all on." Half-kneeling on the seat beside him, she grimly recounted the action.

"Any cars coming?"

"Not a sign. Road's completely empty."

Steven gunned the car round the last curve, zipped down the road across the flat. "Right! We'll be there in a minute. I'll stop in front of the bike. You jump out, go over to the bike, make out you're using the radio. Okay?"

"And you?"

"I'll be busy," said Steven.

At the sound of an approaching car, the three hooligans paused in their game, turned towards the road. Immediately, the traffic officer twisted free, hurled himself at one, bearing him to the ground. A second youth whirled, punching, kicking the uniformed man while the third faced the road belligerently, daring the oncoming driver to interfere.

Steven swept past till he was beyond the motorcycle, braked hard, tumbled out, raced towards the milling group.

"Break it up!" he called sharply. "You're all under arrest."

The dark-haired lout smiled derisively. "Yeah! Says who!" He swung a vicious left at Steven who blocked it with his fore-

99

arm. For a second, Steven dodged wildly-swinging punches then ducked in to hold his assailant in a tight clinch.

"I'm police!" he shouted loud enough for everyone to hear. "Policewoman Watson's calling reinforcements right now. So break it up. There'll be a car here any minute."

Steven's own particular bully boy wrenched himself free, looked towards Kylie who was giving a creditable imitation of radio communication. Steven stood ready to defend himself if the bluff did not work but Darkie was convinced. His cry of alarm triggered the others into flight.

They did not go far. Steven grabbed at Darkie, holding him firmly despite frantic struggles. Out of the corner of his eye, he noted Lance Brendon doing the same.

The traffic officer forced his captive into submission against the hard ground, but the third man reached the wire fence of adjacent farmland. He yelled to his companions to break free but Steven and Lance held grimly to their prizes so the escapee set off cross-country alone.

Brendon hauled his man to his feet, pushed him against the car. "All right, you two!" he snapped. "Get into the car and stay there. No funny business. D'you hear!"

They climbed sullenly into the car, sat staring vacantly over the farmland where their companion disappeared.

"What happened?" asked Steven, breathing heavily.

"Oh, usual thing. Drinking. Throwing bottles on to the road. I stopped them. Driver refused a drink test so I grabbed the key. Then things really started popping."

"They certainly did," said Steven.

Brendon stooped, picked up his helmet, stood with it dangling from his left hand while his right flicked dust from his uniform, rubbed an occasional tender spot. Steven half expected him to bring out a comb but he contented himself with a quick thread through with his fingers.

"You'd better check on your reinforcements," said Steven drily. "I'll keep an eye on these two."

Brendon opened his mouth to say something, read the message in Steven's eyes, said instead, "Yeh. Better give them a shake up, eh?" He went over to the motorcycle, started his relay all the while looking towards the car where Kylie was sitting with averted face.

He finished his message, came back, checked the prisoners once more before leaning casually against the bonnet. "They're on their way. Won't be long." He looked in the direction the escapee had taken. "Pity he got away."

"Not important. You've got two. That'll rope him in. I see you're still on the bike."

"Yes. Get my car back to-morrow. Nothing, they said."

"No. Nothing."

Brendon tilted his head momentarily at the sound of distant sirens, turned back to Steven. "Lucky you came along right then. What're you doing in this neck of the woods?"

"Had to go to Masterton. A case I had coming up before court to-morrow. Jonas said to get out of it."

Brendon smiled knowingly, looked pointedly at the westering sun, Steven's small car, his female companion. Steven could guess what he was thinking. Maybe that made him speak sharply.

"You're a bit out of your territory, too, aren't you?"

"Yeh. Locals all tied up with this Maidstone Park thing. I'm looking after the wide open spaces."

A police car came into sight over the ridge and conversation lapsed. The two captives were transhipped, Brendon handed over the car keys to a constable who immediately turned the jalopy towards Upper Hutt, the police car following.

Brendon smiled at Steven. "You'll be wanting to be on your way, eh? But before you go—" The insolent smile deepened. "This policewoman—Watson, you said her name was. What's she to you?"

"She's my wife," said Steven curtly. "She's never been a policewoman. And her name's not Watson."

A shutter came down over Brendon's eyes as Steven explained Kylie's relationship. "Oh, very clever. Got the point over, too. Still, I'd like to say thank you. She helped us quite a bit."

Steven could think of no escape from that one, led Brendon to the car, opened the door. "This is Traffic Officer Lance Brendon," he said coldly. "He'd like to say thank you."

He stepped back to allow Brendon in front of him. Kylie looked up, her eyes moved to Brendon's face, widened, and a slow warm smile curved her lips. Steven could not see Brendon's face, the words he was speaking seemed commonplace enough but apparently the look that accompanied them was not.

Suddenly Steven felt small and chunky beside Brendon. He was close on six foot but Brendon was at least three inches taller, lean, hungry-looking, the type women seemed to fall for. His tousled appearance did not detract from the smartness of his uniform, the deepening bruise on his left cheek probably added a touch of glamour.

Steven did not allow his feelings to show. He spoke casually about making up lost time. Brendon stepped back to usher him into the driver's seat while Kylie slid over to the passenger side.

He tried to ignore Brendon's look of smug satisfaction as he drove away. And he was careful not to look at Kylie.

They had almost reached the next rise when Kylie gave a little chuckle. "Y'know, Steven. Your traffic officer's quite a man. He didn't say anything much but I swear he was making a pass at me."

"Yeh. Does it all the time, so I hear. Anything in a skirt. Just can't seem to help himself."

"Aha! God's gift to women, eh? Sticks out all over him." She laughed delightedly. "Quite a man!"

"Always thought him a bit effeminate myself," said Steven.

"Effeminate!" crowed Kylie. "With those shoulders?"

"No, but he giggles. And you ought to see him run . . ." His voice trailed as Kylie reached over, placed her hand lightly on his arm. She said nothing but the gentle pressure embraced him.

"Sorry," he said. "Guess I got carried away a bit there."

As he turned the car to take the curve of the hill he glanced back to where Brendon was sitting astride his machine, microphone to his lips, probably reporting to control.

He began to think of the fight. Not much of a fight, he had been in worse, but there was something about Brendon, an eagerness, a wolfishness that had sharpened the contours of his

102

face leaving a kind of ugliness, the face of a man who would welcome the chance to hurt, to maim, to kill.

Was this the face that Blaney had seen when Brendon had "bloodied his nose" over Arline? Had it shocked him as much as it shocked Steven? The not-so-pretty Brendon concealed behind the smiling mask of geniality.

With a start, Steven realized that, despite his brave words to Judy Clark, he had written Brendon off as someone too shallow and mercurial to plan a long-range murder. Now he had seen the underneath Brendon he began to speculate perhaps, maybe. He frowned, wondering how much his thoughts had been coloured by Brendon's blatant approach to Kylie.

When they reached home, Steven paused only long enough to unload the potatoes donated by Kylie's parents, telephone around to find Peacock's whereabouts, then he was back in the car driving to Petone.

Jonas listened quietly to Steven's account of his arrangements about the Masterton case, the negative results of his discussion of their immediate case with Nathan, and finally the fight in the Kaitoke Hills.

He nodded. "Yes, I went to see Arline Muir about that accusation of hers. She withdrew it. Said she was upset. Wanted to lash out at someone. And Brendon deserved it, she says. Too darned unruffled by Blaney's death. What d'you think?"

"Maybe she's got something but he's not the type to brood. Takes life as it comes. Casual on the surface but underneath— who knows?"

"Yes, who knows! By the way, Muir denied she'd mentioned a gun to you."

"Oh, she did, did she? Typical!"

"Maybe Brendon got to her?"

Steven thought that over. Brendon had followed Arline after her hysterical outburst. Had he caught up with her? From the way Judy spoke—

"Maybe but I think there's another explanation for that." He recounted his meeting with Judy Clark.

Peacock rubbed his chin. "So that's it. Now I come to think

103

of it, Judy did seem rather subdued. Well, now they realize Blaney was murdered, maybe we'll have a bit more sense and a little less nonsense in that direction. Pity we can't say that for everyone."

He selected three papers from a pile in front of him. "The first sign of protest. Three old biddies reckon Tommy shouldn't be allowed to roam around endangering people's lives."

Steven read the letters with disgust. "They're acting entirely on hearsay. We've been keeping the Tommy angle under wraps."

Peacock's lips twisted as he replaced the letters. "That type don't need facts! But it gave me an idea. Had a good look through all the papers. To see if there had been any mention of Tommy. And I came across the results of the Bounty Competition. Seen it? A Mrs Dawson won, did you notice?"

He handed the *Sunday Times* to Steven. "It was in the *Sunday News*, too. Rang Cottar straight away. Asked him to save all entries naming Blaney as the gambler. No trouble, he said. Had to keep all entries for a month anyway."

"What will that tell us?"

Jonas smiled tightly, refolded the paper, placed it once more on the table. "Nothing maybe. But I'm curious. Might point to someone we haven't thought of. Cottar says Duffy's got the entries and he's out yachting. But he'll have them for us first thing to-morrow, he says. Let's hope there is something although ——Y'know, I have a funny feeling about this case. A funny feeling. Blaney wasn't in Petone long enough . . ." His voice trailed. He sighed heavily. "No matter. Tommy White's still our only lead. And I can't get at him! They were out all day to-day. Left early this morning. Weren't back last time I called, quarter to seven."

"He'll be back to-morrow."

"Should be. In the middle of exams at the tech. If only we could get White on our side!"

"Maybe he thinks he's protecting Tommy."

"Yes. Or maybe Mrs White." He folded his hands across his chest. "D'you know who Mrs White is—was? Jennifer Sheed."

Steven looked at him blankly. The name meant nothing to

him, yet, from the way Jonas spoke, it seemed he was expected to know.

"Yes. Bob Whittaker told me. Be before your time. Pretty gruesome really. Jeremy Sheed. He was an artist. Mrs White, Jennifer, was a bit of a kid when she married him. One of his students, I believe. They had two kids and she was expecting again."

Steven stared at him, still unable to follow the line of thought but he guessed some tragedy and the last bit was obvious.

"Tommy?" he asked.

"Yes, Tommy. White was Jeremy Sheed's second cousin. Hadn't met Jennifer before. But after. Well, she was in a state of mental shock. Complete. He came down, tried to straighten things out. Managed to persuade her to marry him a few weeks before Tommy was born."

"You still haven't explained," Steven prompted.

Jonas roused himself. "No? Jeremy Sheed, as I said, was an artist. Of course, in those days anyone trying to make a living out of being an artist must've had a hole in his head. Things have changed a lot since then. But Jeremy tried it. Not too successfully, from all accounts."

He clasped his hands behind his head. "I'm not saying he wasn't a good artist, mind you. Some of his work was next door to brilliant, I understand, the more creative stuff. But nobody was interested in those days. He did commercial to keep going and there was this competition for a bank mural. Y'know the kind?"

"They still do it," reminded Steven.

"Well, Jeremy sneered but he entered. So did Jennifer. And she won. Jeremy was furious. Because he was the one with talent. Not Jennifer. He told her to refuse the commission. But Jennifer wouldn't. She'd gone without too long to please his fancies. Now she had a chance to bring in a bit of money, her own money."

Jonas sighed. "She paid in blood. One day towards the end of July, Jennifer went out to confer with the bank officials. She came home and there was Jeremy at the window. He waited till she opened the gate, picked up the two children, one in each

105

arm, so she could see. Next minute the whole place went up in flames."

"He set it alight?"

"Yes. Place was saturated with petrol. Jennifer tried to get in but the doors were locked. Neighbours dragged her away. There wasn't anything anyone could do."

Steven was silent, shaken by the revelation.

"Bob says White was the best thing that ever happened to her. Encouraged her to paint, and now she's one of our greats."

"Amen to that," said Steven. "A really great painter. The other two children were normal, I take it."

"Seems like. A boy of ten months. A girl 22 months."

"That's why Doc Whittaker was so mad. He was trying to protect Mrs White. Professor White, too. Even he sort of——"

"Yes," said Jonas softly. "As I said before, we never really got to talk with Mrs White at all, did we?"

CHAPTER XII

ON MONDAY MORNING, Peacock went straight to Fairbrother to arrange his softening-up tactics for Professor White while Steven checked confirming reports against earlier statements.

The only new information covered the airport hire car. The driver was James Kinlock Dempster, disqualified for twelve months for negligent driving involving the death of a girl. Now, Feilding police would take over, check to make sure that Leybourne was truly unaware that his brother-in-law had his licence.

Peacock came in with a rush. Steven put aside the reports and they set off for their appointment with Jeff Cottar. As they pulled into the factory parking area, they found Cottar waiting. He greeted them heartily, led them to his office where a husky, sun-drenched man was sitting negligently on the corner of a desk.

"Bob Duffy, Manager of the Enzed," said Cottar. "Asked him down to make it legal. The entries are in his custody."

While Duffy acknowledged introductions, Cottar lifted papers from a locked drawer. "This typed list covers all entries naming Blaney as gambler, Inspector. Names and addresses. And this bundle's the actual entries."

"Thanks very much," said Peacock. "Very thoughtful of you."

He began leafing through the entries while Steven took the typed list. There were 50 names on the list. Some would have made guesses, others actually knew Blaney's rôle.

"Police were not allowed to enter?" Steven asked.

"No. Police. Ponderosa Committee. And their families."

"A Mrs Dawson won the bounty. Right?"

"Yes. She's not on that list. Didn't get the gambler. The only entrant to name three out of the four."

Peacock sorted out two entry forms, frowned. He held them against the light, placed them in front of Cottar.

"Would you say they were made out by the same man?"

"Possibly. But different names. One of the rules. Only one entry per person. And we didn't have to disqualify anyone on that account."

"But there's nothing stopping someone using another person's name?"

"Nothing. Except the other person couldn't enter."

"May I have these two entries? Like to have an expert opinion. I'd guess these two signatures were by the same man even though there's been an attempt at disguise."

"Certainly," said Cottar. "We arranged to hold the papers but, of course, circumstances alter cases."

Peacock glanced briefly at the list of names Steven passed to him, turned to the bank manager.

"I read your statement, Mr Duffy. You claimed you didn't know the identity of the gambler."

"That's correct."

"Mr Cottar said only you and he knew the identities of the bandits. Would you like to explain?"

"Simple enough, Inspector. Jeff and I did sort out three but the fourth one, well, he was chosen by police, not us. By the time they'd made their decision the whole matter was in Jeff's hands. I'd moved on to something else. We were fighting against time, Inspector. Had to do everything in around ten days. While the publicity was hot. So we were up to our eyes. All of us."

"And on no occasion did Mr Cottar mention the name of the police selectee to you?"

"Wouldn't say that. Could be it was mentioned. But I didn't know Blaney. So I'm afraid the name didn't click. Had too many other things on my mind."

"Yes, I can understand that."

Peacock thanked the two men, left with Steven to go back to the police car. As they drove off, he examined the prepared list,

108

the two maverick entries, finally folded the papers, placed them in his inside pocket.

"Quite a wad of entries from Hudson House, weren't there?" he said conversationally. "Seems they all knew about Blaney. Better check those statements again. See how many admitted it."

"The name that surprised me was Judd Cumming."

"Ah, yes, Cumming. I think we'll have a little chat with him. Right away. Know where he lives?"

"Yes. He's got a bach at the back of a house on Koro Koro Crescent."

"Where was he Friday? The hospital, wasn't it?"

"Yes. Got stuck by a wild pig about six months ago. Left leg. Gets treatment regularly every month."

Steven drove through Jackson Street noting Ponderosa Day notices still in evidence. Here and there wisps of straw floated around shop fronts. As fast as one accumulation was blown away another would be collected by the restive breeze.

They found Cumming at home, hanging laundry on a line set aside for his own use. He did not seem surprised to see them, continued pegging with a brief, "Won't be a minute".

Steven and Peacock waited, looking around with interest. The neat bach was set far enough away from the main house to seem almost private. A small clump of wallflowers by the door filled the air with cloying sweetness but it was the flourishing vegetable garden that stirred Steven's envy. There was even an asparagus bed beyond the double row of thick-stemmed tomato vines.

The old man finished his task, fussily put away his peg basket before giving his attention to his visitors.

"Would you like to sit in the sun or come inside?"

They opted to use the garden seat built against the bach and Cumming brought out a kitchen chair for himself. He looked at them inquiringly and Peacock did not waste time.

"How did you know Joe Blaney was to be a bandit?"

Cumming spread one hand slightly, placed it back on his knee. "Why not? Open secret as far as I can understand." He grinned impishly. "You obviously don't know that Ed Sigley's my brother-in-law."

109

"No, we didn't know that," said Peacock. "Why don't you live at Hudson House?"

Cumming shook his head. "Not me. I like my independence. Ed and I get on better the less we see of each other. But it was all planned there, y'know. They have a kind of bull session—Tuesdays, Thursdays. I just happened to be there when they were talking about it."

"And you told Tommy White?"

The old man paused, looked down at his hands resting on his knees. "Yes. I told Tommy." He looked up again, a stricken look on his face. "I told Tommy the whole set-up. The sheriff to take three. The other to get away. I explained it was all acting. The men might look dead but they really weren't. I told him several times because Tommy forgets so quickly."

He rubbed his hand along his left leg, examined the palm minutely while waiting for them to speak.

Peacock frowned. "How much did Tommy understand, d'you think? Enough to plan ahead. To go along to the hideout. Wait?"

"No!" Cumming shook his head vigorously. "I told Tommy what was going to happen. In detail, yes, but only what he was likely to see. I never said anything about Gregg's."

"You think someone else supplied the missing information, arranged for Tommy to be there at the right moment?"

"Has to be that way. Tommy hasn't any sense of time."

"All right. Now, you said you don't visit Hudson House too often. Why that particular day? To see your brother-in-law?"

"No. I—I went to see Keith Hounsell." He sighed. "Tommy's bedroom. Overlooks Hounsell's room. And Hounsell has guns. Tommy told me about these guns. He'd watched Hounsell clean them often enough. He was interested."

"Naturally," said Peacock in the brief pause.

"His father has guns. Lets him play with them. Could he play with Hounsell's guns? Look at them anyway. Of course, this didn't come out quite as straightforward as that. Only bits and pieces. Talked about it so much I began to get worried."

"Why didn't you mention it to his father?"

Cumming gave a short laugh. "Professor White! D'you think

110

he'd come down to ground long enough to take notice! No, I thought if I warned Hounsell, he'd clean them elsewhere. And Tommy would soon forget."

"Did you see Hounsell?"

"No. He'd gone away that morning."

"So this was last Tuesday. Who was there?"

"Well, Ed. Couple of the boarders. That tow-headed cop, Bruce someone or other, and that Brendon fella."

"Gambling?"

"Card playing. Not gambling. Ed's a bit pious on that one. Sits in to make sure."

Steven picked up the race book lying on the bench. "You like a gamble yourself, Mr Cumming. Go to the races often?"

"Haven't been on a course since Lady Tinkle won the double. A couple of bets at the TAB. That's my limit."

Peacock intervened. "Getting back to that bull session. They were discussing Ponderosa Day. Planning the robbery?"

"No. They'd fixed that. We were just talking generally."

"And Blaney in particular."

"Well, yes, I suppose so."

"Now, about Tommy. You did say you'd do your best to find out who told him to go to Gregg's. Any luck?"

"No. Didn't get anywhere. Tommy just blanked out. Didn't want to talk. And you can't make him, y'know.

"His parents haven't been able to reach him either."

Cumming gazed shrewdly at them. "Means you call in the experts. They do it with hypnotism and stuff, don't they?"

"Maybe. But that means getting Professor White's co-operation. Unfortunately the good doctor believes Tommy did it."

Cumming blinked. "Don't you think he did it?"

"We know quite well he didn't do it, Mr Cumming."

The old man expelled a deep breath. "Well, that's something! I think most people——" He glanced at his watch. "Anything more I can do for you, gentlemen. I have an appointment I must keep at ten-thirty. And it's ten now."

Peacock shook his head. As they were turning the corner of the path, Steven looked back but Cumming had already disappeared.

"Nice garden. And he seems comfortable enough."

"That close to the railway line? Wonder he gets any sleep!"
Steven laughed. "An old railway man like Cumming! Probably can't sleep without a few trains chugging up and down."

At the station, Peacock went in to see if the Professor White arrangements had been completed while Steven waited in the car. And waited. Finally he wandered in himself.

He found a mild state of rebellion, one uniform man speaking into the telephone, four others standing in a muttering group. After one swift glance, Steven went to the front office.

Peacock was gazing out of the window at the drab houses on the other side of the street, hands clasped behind him, tell-tale flush of anger on his cheeks. He turned when Steven entered.

"Thought they'd found him!" he barked.

"Found him?" inquired Steven blandly.

"Dr White! They 'phoned earlier and he said—he said he didn't have time for charades. Charades! Doesn't he realize——" Bitterly he slapped one balled fist into the palm of his other hand. "And now he's disappeared. Nobody can locate him. I've told them to stay on the 'phone, harry them till he turns up again."

Steven could imagine panic stations at the institute with this constant 'phoning but it was five-past-eleven before the report came that White was back in his office.

"At last," said Peacock. "And Mrs Gregg won't be home?"

"No, sir. She gave us the spare key."

"Right. Get round there, all of you. Set things up. I'll bring Dr White." His instructions to Steven were equally terse. "Drop me at the tech. White and I'll walk down. Give us time to let the steam out."

When Steven arrived at Gregg's, he noticed the arthritic Mrs Davidson at her window, unashamedly interested in the actions of police personnel. They waited patiently till Peacock and White turned into the part-street, the inspector chatting amiably, White looking like a ruffled cockatiel.

Peacock paused by a uniform man standing in the middle of the drive. "All ready?" he asked.

The officer saluted. "Yes, sir. Exactly as you said, sir."

112

Peacock led White to the back of the house. He pointed to the corner of the patio, behind the flourishing hydrangea.

"That's where Tommy waited," he said quietly. "Five minutes. Ten. No longer. He found a key on the patio flagstones, buried it here under the hydrangea, marked it with some marigolds. And see where the sand has built up in the corner. He played with it, drawing patterns with a stem from that bush."

He stepped out on to the drive. "All right. We're ready. Will you stand there, Professor. Out of the way."

He motioned to the corner of the patio. White complied, head tilted at the sound of running feet.

The man who had been waiting in the middle of the drive ran past, reached the bottom of the stairs leading to the flat, turned to ascend. His foot was hardly on the third step when Peacock called loudly, "Bang, you're dead".

The man stopped, whirled, surprise on his face as he leaned against the banister. Apparently Peacock had not forewarned him, relying on natural reaction to obtain the effect he wanted.

"All right. Stay there," he said sharply. "And keep perfectly still. We won't be long."

He turned to White. "Tommy was there. Now, crouch down to Tommy's height." The professor crouched down, looked towards the man on the stair. "Now, aim a pistol at him."

White half rose to his feet. "Inspector, this is——"

Peacock silenced him. "Just do this, please. Just this one thing. That's all I ask."

White looked at him angrily, resumed his crouched position, aimed an imaginary gun. Steven was interested to note the careful stance, left arm crooked, gun hand resting on the support.

"He couldn't have missed from here. Even if he wasn't used to the gun. A lucky shot."

"Yes," said Peacock softly. "But the angle of the bullet. Did you know the trajectory was almost horizontal?"

White straightened. "But that's impossible. Tommy couldn't——"

"Not Tommy. From where Tommy was it was quite impossible as you say. Now, let's go indoors."

He motioned the man on the stair to stay put, led White into

113

the narrow kitchen, placed a chair against the bench. "Here, climb up there. Look out of the fanlight. The right hand one."

White looked at him speculatively, climbed on to the bench, crouched to peer through the narrow gap. He placed his arm along the lower frame, rested his other hand on it in a firing position. He did it twice before he nodded, climbed down.

"Almost horizontal," he said in a subdued voice. "And you have proof a man was in here?"

"Not proof, I'm afraid. Scuff marks on the bench. The ledge there perfectly free from dust. Maybe not even relevant but suggestive when the trajectory is taken into consideration."

White had the grace to look humble. "I apologize, Inspector. To be frank, well, I thought you were setting Tommy up as a scapegoat. That's why—I'm sorry. I thought I was protecting him. What now? Place Tommy in the hands of the experts? Try to bypass the block?"

"It might work. Hope so, because we believe Tommy did see this man at some stage. Only he can identify him."

They were walking along the drive, White expounding his plan to induce Tommy to communicate. Suddenly he stopped, looked around, stooped to pick up the gun lying conspicuously on the chipped bricks, a plastic gun, very much like the real thing.

"Yes, of course," he said softly. "That could be how it happened. Fellow must've come out the front, left the gun on the drive for Tommy to pick up."

He looked back towards the garage. "Can't see the end of the stairs from here, but where Tommy was—he'd see Blaney fall and when nothing else happened, he'd lose interest, wander away. He'd see the gun lying there. Naturally he'd pick it up."

"Naturally."

"I wish I'd realized this earlier. All this time wasted."

He opened his mouth to launch another observation, stopped at the sound of his name being called urgently. The three men swung round and Steven felt a prickle of fear chill his skin.

A uniform man was standing by Mrs White, half-supporting her as she leaned against the fence. Small and remote she had seemed before, now only the husk remained, all life, all animation fled.

114

As one, they hurried to the footpath, White reaching her first, standing quietly before her, his hand gentle on her shoulder.

"What is it, m'dear?" he asked. Mrs White lifted pain filled eyes, tried to speak. "Breathe deeply. Go on. There's my girl."

The woman did as she was told, leaning against him for comfort. "It's Tommy. He's gone. Oh, he's gone. I went to his room —and Alex—he's gone. Gone."

CHAPTER XIII

THEY DROVE THE Whites home, walked them to the door. As soon as they were inside, Peacock said, "First we search the house".

"That's hardly necessary, Inspector. I assure you—"

"Routine, Professor. We always do it this way."

White flinched at Peacock's brusqueness, retired to the kitchen. Peacock jerked a thumb at Steven. "Upstairs. I'll do down here."

Steven raced upstairs, worked his way round the stair well. The first north-side room had been converted into a studio. Steven's brief survey took in the half-finished canvas, a native bush background, tall trees looped with fairy moss. He wondered fleetingly what was planned for the space at the base of a massive totara. An antler-hung stag? A woodsman's axe? Probably nothing so crude. Jenny White used more subtle touches for her effects.

Tommy's room was next, more of a playroom with a bed than a bedroom in the accepted sense. Steven surveyed the toys, apparatus, with a feeling of sadness.

After a routine close search, he leaned out of the window, examined Tommy's "mountain". The creeper was thick and gnarled in places, strong enough to carry Tommy's light weight, the blue gleam of metal steps bridging gaps. At the foot of the mountain lay a toy cabin cruiser which could have been left there to-day—or yesterday.

Steven looked thoughtfully at Hudson House, so close, so remote. He could see into Hounsell's room, part of the bed, the wicker chair, the Parker Hale leaning carelessly against it.

The blind was down in one of the back-to-back windows

116

directly opposite. Heath's room? Asleep? Not disturbed by the slight sound of Tommy climbing down the creeper?

The bathroom, then the south-side rooms—a spare room containing theatrical paraphernalia, costumes, mock-up sets, out of date posters; and the master bedroom, surprisingly austere, unadorned after the indulgence of Tommy's room, the tinsel of the theatre room.

Steven met Peacock at the foot of the stairs, reported the cabin cruiser below the mountain. "He'd been playing in the bathroom. Bath part full of water, toy boats all over."

Peacock nodded. "No luck down here, either. Thought maybe the gun room. Fascinating place. Kid could amuse himself there all day. No trouble."

They turned into the kitchen-cum-living room where Mrs White was lying on the wide windowseat, one arm flung over her eyes. As soon as they entered, she swung her feet around, sat upright.

"No need to disturb yourself," said Peacock gruffly.

"No, no. I feel better this way." She leaned forward, passing her hand briefly over her eyes then sat still, waiting.

"When did you last see Tommy?" Peacock asked.

"Early this morning. About half past nine. I heard Mr Hounsell calling him a little earlier, quarter past maybe."

"Hounsell? From next door?"

"Yes. I heard this 'Tommy, Tommy,' so I went round. He was there, against the fence. Holding one of his guns. And asking Tommy to come down and have a look at it."

"And Tommy?"

"Tommy? He was leaning out of his window. I'm afraid I was cross with Mr Hounsell. I—I told him we were keeping Tommy indoors and we didn't want him interfering with our arrangements."

"And Hounsell?"

"Well, he was very apologetic. Said he knew Tommy was interested in guns. Thought he could show them to him. I—I can't remember his exact words. But something like that. And I said—I said—Tommy was ill. Leave him alone."

"And did he?"

117

"Well, yes. He was very apologetic, as I said. Hoped Tommy would be better soon. Asked me to tell him he could come to look at the guns any time. Then he went off."

"And you?"

"I went up to talk to Tommy. Try to talk to him, that is. He usually does communicate but lately——" She waved her hand helplessly. "He just looks at you. It's all this questioning. Not just you, Inspector. I'm afraid we're just as guilty. And then, on top of that, I kept him indoors."

"You think that's why he went off?"

"It must be. Oh, it's all my fault! I could've taken him out. I could've taken him down to the beach. Let him have a swim. I could've taken him to the wharf so he could fish. Nothing I was doing was so important. Nothing!"

"There's no need to distress yourself, Mrs White," soothed Peacock. "As far as we know at this juncture, Tommy is all right. The whole force is looking for him so if he's just gone——"

Mrs White shook her head wearily. "But we don't know, do we? He could've been gone anything up to two hours now. If Mr Cumming hadn't come——"

"Cumming was here?"

"Yes. Just before twelve. I was—I was in the studio and I came down. Mr Cumming wanted to take Tommy fishing but I said, no, he wasn't allowed to go anywhere. Mr Cumming seemed surprised at first then he said perhaps that was best."

"That was when you found Tommy missing?"

"Yes. I thought I'd make a picnic lunch. Take it up and have it with Tommy in his bedroom. He usually liked that. And we often do that when he's not—well. But when I went up to his room he was gone. Gone! Then I thought of what Mr Cumming had said and I was frightened. Terribly frightened."

Peacock frowned. "What exactly did Cumming say?"

"Well, he told me not to let Tommy out of my sight. I didn't worry then as Tommy had to pass the studio door to come downstairs. I never thought he'd—I never thought——"

"Naturally. But we still haven't established when he did go, Mrs White. It might not be as long as you think. For instance, Tommy was playing with his boats——"

118

He stopped abruptly when Mrs White shook her head.

"He didn't play with them. I filled the bath, brought out his boats. Tried to get him interested. But he refused." She shrugged. "Can you blame him? That's what I do to keep him amused on a wet day."

Peacock was silent, then he sighed noisily, stood up. "Thanks, Mrs White. We'll leave it at that meantime. You did say you'd been questioning Tommy again. Any success?"

"No, Inspector. Tommy doesn't talk to us any more."

Peacock turned to White who went over to his wife, "Lie down again, Jenny. Lie down."

Mrs White lay back obediently and White led the two men out into the hall. "Anything I can do, Inspector?"

"Not right now, I'm afraid. We've sent out a full alert. We'll let you know as soon as we hear anything."

White nodded, closed the door softly after them.

Peacock was thoughtful as he strode along the path to the gate. He paused briefly at the car to send a terse message in to locate Cumming, then turned towards Hudson House.

When they rang the bell by the usually-open door, there was no response, no sounds to indicate anyone was moving in the mute depths. They wandered around the back but the only signs of life were some smalls pegged to a side line. Peacock poked around the yard, looked into the workshop, even went through the back gate, along the narrow lane to the recreation grounds. The grounds were empty except for a solitary policeman hurrying along the outward track.

"Oh, well. Might as well go back."

Cumming was waiting for them when they arrived. A cruising car had found him on Tennyson Street so the car sent to his house was recalled.

"And what were you doing in Tennyson Street?" Peacock asked amiably.

"Went along to have a yarn with Joby Riley. He lives in Tennyson Street with his daughter."

"Did you see Joby?"

The old man shook his head. "No. Not at home."

119

"Did you know young Tommy White is missing?"

"Tommy? But when I went around there——How long has he been gone?" he demanded, suddenly intensely angry.

"We don't know exactly. Maybe two to three hours. Maybe only half an hour. Where'd you think he'd go Mr Cumming? If he wanted to run away?"

"Tommy wouldn't run away," Cumming responded absently.

"No? It's a lovely day. Tommy always goes out to play fine days. And to-day he was being kept indoors. For his own protection. But would he realize that? We think he climbed down his creeper ladder."

Cumming studied the ceiling, looked around at the window, finally shook his head. "No. Something I never thought the youngun would do. Probably just wanted to get out of the house, I'd say. I suppose you've been to the beach?"

"Yes. Sent a man down straight away. No luck so far. Would he go fishing?"

"Not by himself. But he could watch. Maybe the wharf. Or the estuary bridge. Then there's the sandhills. Down east end. And he's got a fort in the brush on the other side of McEwan Park. You have to look pretty hard to find it."

"What about the boatsheds?"

Cumming shook his head. "No, he wouldn't go into a shed. Even if the door was left open."

Peacock looked at him sharply. "Normally maybe. But now? Perhaps he's resentful. Even angry. Then ordinary behaviour patterns might not apply. We've found from experience that concealment seems to be their first desire. So—the boatsheds?"

Cumming nodded. "Yes. That sounds logical. But for my money I'd say the fort. If Tommy wanted to disappear, that'd be where he'd go."

He looked expectantly at Peacock who nodded. "Right. We'll have a look. There's a car waiting outside. Tell the men where you want to go."

Steven took Cumming to the car, instructed the crew to go wherever the old man told them. When he returned, Peacock was replacing the receiver.

"Notified Lower Hutt," he said grimly. "They're rounding up

120

extra men, contacting Trentham for dogs. Just in case."

"What's the deadline?"

"Three o'clock. We can't move too soon. We daren't leave it too late." He picked up a pencil, began to twiddle it between his fingers. "Should've foreseen that, I suppose. But I let myself be fooled by the fact they were keeping Tommy close to protect him from us."

"You couldn't guess he'd take off on his own bat."

"Should've thought of it, though. Taken precautions. Now he's vulnerable. If we don't reach him first . . ."

He paused and Steven said drily, "If you'd put a guard on the house, White would've raised the roof."

"Yeh, I guess so." But he still seemed unhappy.

"At least, it's accomplished something. Mrs White's come out of the shadows. Talked quite freely there."

"Nothing relevant though. We still have to talk to her about Blaney. Not yet, of course. Tidy this up first."

"And she won't be a hostile witness now."

Peacock eyed him dourly. "Think not? If anything's happened to Tommy, maybe she'll blame us."

Moorhead knocked, poked his head round the door. "That car with Cumming just called in. No sign of Tommy at the fort. Going to do a close search of the immediate area, trails and hideyholes all over the place. Then they'll move on to the boatsheds."

Peacock nodded and Moorhead withdrew. "Didn't expect anything else. Bit too easy. Oh well, we still have to talk to Hounsell. Let's go."

Keith Hounsell was not in and Sigley did not know where he was. He invited the two men in with sour grace, led the way to the kitchen where he was fixing a belated lunch for himself.

"Anyone else at home?" Peacock asked.

"Blokes upstairs probably. Sleeping."

"What time did they go to bed?"

"How would I know? Usual time, I expect."

"The usual time's around eight in the morning, isn't it?"

"Not on Monday. After the weekend, y'see. They just get a bit of kip to take them through the night."

"And you can't actually say when? Does that mean you weren't here? You don't usually go out Mondays, do you?"

"Not usually," Sigley bristled. "But I had to see my lawyer this morning. Don't like the way things are shaping."

"Oh? In what particular way?"

"This gun business. Wanted to know if I was liable."

"And are you?"

"Not according to David Rawles. But he's going to do a bit more investigation before he finally advises."

"Cautious type, eh? What time did you leave, Mr Sigley?"

"Eleven or thereabouts. Didn't take too much notice."

"Pity. We may need to know exactly." He ignored Sigley's petulant grimace. "Tommy White's missing. If anything's happened, we'll be checking on everyone. Everyone in the street."

Sigley began to bluster, stopped as Keith Hounsell came into the room, looked inquiringly at the three men.

"Good afternoon, Mr Hounsell," said Peacock quietly. "We came to see you about Tommy White."

Hounsell stiffened. "What about Tommy White?" he demanded.

"Did you know he's disappeared?"

"How in hell—!" he started, paused, looked at them more closely. "Something up, is there?" he asked.

"Hope not. But it is possible."

Hounsell swung on his heel, dashed from the room. Peacock looked at Steve, followed. They found Hounsell muttering to himself as he unlocked his bedroom door. He flung it open, relaxed.

"It's still there. Thank God for that!" He entered, placed the Parker Hale back on its rack. "Gave me a bad moment there. Thought he'd got hold of another one of my guns."

"I told you to get those guns out of here!" Sigley's harsh voice rasped through the ensuing silence.

Hounsell strode swiftly to the door, snarled, "Shut your fat face. What I've got in my room's my own business."

122

Sigley yelled an obscenity at Hounsell who answered as profanely but the developing slanging match stopped abruptly at the sound of thumping from the upper floor.

Tight-lipped, Sigley threw himself at Hounsell who held him firmly at arm's length. Frantically the smaller man struggled to reach his adversary with wildly swinging fists till Hounsell gave him a hard shove which sent him staggering.

"Get lost, little man," he sneered. "You might get hurt."

Quickly, Peacock stepped between the two men. "All right. Fun's over. We'd like your undivided attention, Mr Hounsell."

Hounsell glanced mockingly at Sigley, led the way into his room, shut the door.

"Hardly intelligent behaviour," said Peacock drily. "He can always get his own back by turfing you out."

"Oh, he'll get over it. Blows his top all the time. Nobody takes any notice. Take a pew." He sat on the edge of the bed, took out a packet of tobacco, began to roll a cigarette. "What's this about Tommy White?" he asked mildly as though the little scene with Sigley had never happened.

"Let's begin with this morning, shall we?" said Peacock. "Mrs White says you were calling Tommy just after nine. Right?"

Hounsell licked the edge of the paper, smoothed it down. "Yeh. Thought I'd show him my guns. Chat him up a bit. If I could get him talking, maybe he'd let slip something about the Luger. Maybe."

"Have you ever talked to Tommy before?"

"Not much. 'Hi, there,' and 'How you're doing, young fellow'. That kind of thing. He's a bit, well, lacking. But sometimes if you can find something they're interested in——" He shrugged. "Just a thought. Didn't work, though. Mrs White came along, bawled me out. Interfering, she said."

Peacock said blandly, "Mrs White said Tommy was ill."

Hounsell smiled grimly. "Ill, nothing! Locked in his bedroom, more like. How'd he get out? Down the creeper?"

"Yes. You knew Tommy used the creeper as a ladder?"

"Sure. Guess we all did. First time I saw him nearly had tomtits. Thought he'd fall for certain."

"Have you seen Tommy since then, Mr Hounsell?"

"No. After that little fiasco I went up town, couple of shops, then down to the rowing club."

"Well, let us know the approximate times you were any place, witnesses and so on. We may need to check."

Hounsell's eyes narrowed. "Hey, what's this? The kid's likely to walk in any moment."

Peacock regarded him gravely, sighed audibly. "Mr Hounsell, we are concerned by Tommy's absence. So concerned that we have pulled every man jack off the Blaney case to help in the search. Instructions are to notify me as soon as he's located. Yet no one's tried to contact me, Mr Hounsell. No one."

CHAPTER XIV

THE SEARCH PATTERN was in full operation, dogs and handlers, reinforcements from all close divisions.

Steven sat over his map, marking results as they came to hand. The beach, negative. The wharf, negative. Sand dunes, negative. Raceway. Parks. Playing areas. Grandstands. The Tip. Empty sections. Empty houses.

The afternoon lengthened. Steven felt drowsy, drugged by the heat, by the monotonous negative reports, so that he did not immediately grasp the significance of what Peacock was saying on the telephone.

"Yes, Dr White. You're quite right. It's a definite lead. Now, what boats did you say were missing? I see. A small cabin cruiser, battery driven. And a yacht, about fifteen inches."

They knew where the cabin cruiser was, which left the yacht. Orders went out. Check all areas of still water, anywhere a toy yacht could be sailed.

The telephone: "Matheson, sir. House to house. Second time around. A Mrs Allen. Been in town all day. Just got back. Says she saw Tommy on Emerson Street at three minutes past ten. Yes. Looked at the clock as she left. Catching a bus. Yes, he had the yacht. No. Quite alone."

"Mrs Allen there? Put her on. Now, think carefully, Mrs Allen. You're absolutely certain Tommy was alone?"

"Oh, yes, definitely alone. I live half way. Tommy was coming towards me. No one else in sight."

"The way you were facing. What about behind you?"

The woman hesitated. "No. I'm sure, no, wait a minute. There was someone. A man. On the other side. Turning into William

125

Street. A policeman, I think. Yes, a policeman. Y'see, I spoke to Tommy as I went by. He usually says 'hello' back but to-day, well, he kind of cringed away from me. Hurried past. I suppose I should've stopped, talked to him, but I didn't have much time. I did look back at him. Wondering if he was all right, y'know. That's when I saw this man. Out of the corner of my eye sort of, if you know what I mean. Yes, a policeman, I think. No, can't be positive. Just an impression. The clothes probably. Y'know what I mean. Dark trousers. Blue grey shirt, or jacket even. No. Bareheaded. Hair? Don't remember. Lightish, I think. But I wouldn't swear. Wasn't taking too much notice, I'm afraid. Didn't know it was important."

"It might not be. But everything helps. Thanks very much, Mrs Allen. At least, we now know the way Tommy was going. Put Matheson on, will you, please?"

Matheson's deep voice returned. "Matheson here, sir. Any further instructions."

"Yes, pin her down on that description. Why did she think it was a policeman? Make her think about it."

He cradled the telephone, eyes narrowed. "Pull in all parties west of Kensington Avenue. Concentrate on the east end. All areas with water. We've only a few hours of daylight left."

At seven, one of the skin divers searching the river near the old bridge brought up a transistor radio, positively identified as the one stolen from Hounsell's room.

Peacock looked at Steven, nodded. "All right. We'll go have a look. Give someone else a go with the chart."

Steven went thankfully out into the evening air, drove the grey police car to where Jackson Street ended at the riverbank, parked beside the gaily decorated van of Underwater Supplies Ltd.

As they watched, a diver surfaced, waded through the chest high water, handed a small object to the constable kneeling on the bank. They examined the depth gauge while the diver hauled himself on to the bank, pulled off goggles, rubber cap.

Steven felt a jolt of surprise to find it was Keith Hounsell yet he knew the local force had no official divers, relying on the underwater club to supply divers when needed.

126

"Part of the stuff from Hounsell's room," grunted Peacock. "Been identified?"

"Yes. It's definitely mine."

Peacock's head jerked up. He looked at the speaker with slitted eyes. "Got it all?"

"Not all of it. Probably still down there. Visibility practically nil." He gestured towards the slanting sun.

Peacock stood hefting the gauge in his hand, his gaze on the murky water, while Hounsell pulled at his wetsuit to let out the thin film of water warmed now to body heat.

"He didn't want this stuff," mused Peacock. "Took it to cover the theft of the Luger."

"Seems like!" Hounsell stood frowning as though undecided whether to continue the search or to change.

"Sir!" Peacock turned at the urgent summons from the man handling communications. "Sir, they've found Tommy White!"

"Alive?" Peacock demanded harshly.

"No, sir. Drowned. At the stopbank. Behind the school."

Peacock sagged visibly. "Right. Pack up. Call everyone in. And I want to talk to Cumming. And, yes, those shift fellows from Hudson House. Catch them before they go to work."

Steven drove down Jackson Street, turned right at the first cross street, from there into Tennyson Street. Sergeant McCulloch of Lower Hutt was waiting by the entrance of the gravel drive separating the brick pumping station from the old croquet lawn, now knee-high in grass. He led them past the disused club house to a group waiting on the riverbank.

Peacock knelt to lift the light covering from the small body. "No signs of violence?" he asked, straightening.

"Nothing obvious. Could be he did drown."

Peacock scowled. "D'you really think so?"

McCulloch shook his head. "No. Too convenient."

Peacock grunted, looked around. This part of the riverbank was screened from direct observation on the right by the croquet pavilion, corrugated iron over glassless windows.

The grey bulk of the pumping station took care of the left. Further on, extending to the curve of the stopbank, was a patch of secondgrowth heavily impregnated with blackberry, fennel, traversed by well-worn tracks of yellow clay.

"Where did you find him?" Peacock asked.

"You can see better from over there," said McCulloch. He walked into the secondgrowth, pushing aside encroaching branches, turned into a cross path dropping steeply to the water's edge. Steven stayed under the trees concealing the stopbank from the houses on Tennyson Street, watched the others half slide down to a small flattened area jutting out to form a natural backwash.

"This would be where he came. He could sail his boat here without any fear of losing it. But if he fell in from this ledge, you'd expect to find him down there." He indicated the opaque depths beneath the shelf. "He wasn't. He was tangled in that." He pointed to where the bank had subsided so that the tangled mass seemed to be growing from the bottom of the river.

Peacock frowned. "The current?"

"No current." McCulloch glanced briefly at the water lying sullenly motionless between ledge and tangle. "On the other hand, if he went off this ledge here—"

He scrambled along a sloping path once used to reach the top of the bank but now wiped out by the landslide, stood where it ended directly above the drowned secondgrowth.

Peacock nodded, staring morosely at the water.

Where the narrow channel shelved on to Gear Island, isolated clumps of ragwort grew on the stony beach stretching to the row of poplars edging the golf course. Through the trees a scarlet pennant fluttered from the pin.

"The only place overlooking," said Peacock sourly. "And anyone playing would be too busy watching the ball."

He clambered up the bank, stood momentarily amongst the man-high brush gauging chances of observation. "All right. He had to come along Tennyson Street to get here. Maybe someone saw him passing. And those flats down there, where the river curves. Could be someone looked this way at the right time. Could be."

He pointed to the south where the back balconies of flats on Jackson Street stared emptily, too far away for an identification.

128

The ambulance had arrived while they were inspecting the stopbank and Dr Whittaker waited glumly.

"All right," said Peacock. "What's the verdict?"

Whittaker shrugged. "Drowned. No doubt about it. Six to eight hours. D'you mind if I tell Mrs White?"

Peacock agreed readily. "We're treating this as murder until you've definitely proved otherwise."

Whittaker nodded. "I'll bear that in mind."

At the office they found Cumming waiting once again. He looked older, less erect, eyes dull and sunken.

"Sit down," said Peacock gently, quickly proffering a chair. "You know about Tommy, Mr Cumming?"

"Yes. They told me."

"Tommy apparently climbed down the creeper, went straight to the stopbank. When we asked you for suggestions about where Tommy might be, you never once mentioned the stopbank."

"Tommy didn't go to the stopbank by himself. It's a rule."

"Oh, yes. These rules. He'd already broken one rule—going out without telling anyone—yet it didn't occur to you that he might break another. By going to the stopbank?"

Cumming shook his head helplessly.

"And supposing he wasn't alone, Mr Cumming? Then it wouldn't be against the rules, would it?"

The old man's head lifted, eyes wondering. "You mean——"

"I mean someone suggested going over to the stopbank to sail his boat. Someone who knew how to talk to him."

"Yes. Of course. It had to be that way. But who?"

"That's the point, Mr Cumming. Who?" Peacock paused deliberately. "When you were picked up this morning you were in Tennyson Street. Right next to the stopbank."

"Yes, I told you. Went round to see Joby Riley." The old man seemed unaware of the significance of Peacock's remark.

"But Joby Riley wasn't home, was he? Hasn't been home this last fortnight. Been staying with his son at New Plymouth."

"That's right. Supposed to come home yesterday."

"Did you see anyone you knew?"

129

"No. No one home at Joby's. But the people next door. They were home. Might've seen me."

"What about in the street? Did you see anyone?"

"Not a soul. Lunchtime. Could hear the kids up at the school but the street was empty. No, I never saw anyone."

"Did you go over to the stopbank, Mr Cumming?"

"No." A slight shudder passed through him. "Could I have saved him? If I'd gone?"

"No. We know Tommy was on Emerson Street at ten. We know a man close by was wearing dark trousers, blue grey jacket."

Cumming looked down at his dark grey trousers, blue check jacket. "Not me, Inspector. You were with me at ten. And that description. Fit dozens of men in Petone. These jackets were specials at Clausen's end-of-season sale."

"All right, Mr Cumming. We'll leave it at that." He looked at Steven. "Arrange for a car to take him home."

Steven led Cumming from the room, settled him in the car which arrived with the three shift workers.

Thompson was first. He slouched into the room, shirt open to hairy navel, jacket hooked negligently over left shoulder. He slumped fatly into the chair, stared at Peacock.

"I see you patronized Clausen's sale," Peacock began.

Thompson frowned, pulled the jacket round for puzzled scrutiny, recognized the gentleness of the opening gambit, relaxed. "Yeh. We all got one. Good buy. Look here, Inspector. Hope you're not too long. Gotta be at work by eight-thirty. Your blokes picked us up on the corner. Y'know. Where we wait for Stacey's van."

Peacock nodded. "We've arranged alternative transport, Mr Thompson. And I don't think we'll be keeping you long. Just checking on everyone's whereabouts this morning."

"Didn't do much. Bit of washing. Then I wandered up town. Shopping. Had a drink at the pub. Probably can't prove I was any place any time." He frowned. "This got anything to do with young Tommy White? Drowned, wasn't he? Least that's what I heard."

"Every indication is that he was drowned," said Peacock.

130

"At the stopbank! Not enough water to drown a fly!"

"Enough to drown Tommy White. When were you last there?"

"Coupla years. Must be. When I first came to this burg. Used to roam around a bit. New territory, y'see."

"But you don't roam so much now?"

"Nah. Seen it all. Anyway, what's it got to do with me?"

"We're trying to trace Tommy's movements. You live next door. Maybe you saw him this morning?"

"Sure. I saw him. Earlyish. Heard Keith Hounsell and Mrs White having a bit of a barney so I looked out. The kid was at his window then."

"Did you see him after that?"

"Nah. Went down to do this bit of washing like I said. Then I was out in the yard, sitting in the sun a whiles."

"Anyone else there?"

"Yeh. Sonny, Sonny Bristowe. Sunbathing against the back porch. Out of the wind. Sat on the porch right by him."

"Then you went up town. What time did you get back?"

"Oh, about one. Had some grub then turned in for a dose of sleep before to-night."

"Sleep well?"

"Nah. Always hard on Monday. And that racket downstairs. Hey! Did you know about that, Inspector. Siggy and Hounsell were slanging it out real hot."

"We were there when it happened."

The bright gleam in Thompson's eyes died. "Oh, didn't know that. No right to keep those damn guns there anyways. Nuts that guy. Spends all his dough on hunting gear."

"What d'you spend your money on?" Peacock asked gently.

Thompson almost snarled, recovered to say stiffly, "I'm separated, Inspector. Takes a bit of moulah to pay maintenance."

"Mr Thompson, how well did you know Tommy White?"

Thompson rubbed his chin. "Well, he lives next door, y'know. Tried to talk to him coupla times. No soap. Not much good at this baby talk stuff myself."

"Ever see anyone else talk to him? Anyone you know?"

131

"Well, lotsa guys say hello. Comes natural to some guys."

"You mean the men at Hudson House?"

"Yeh. Saturdays. Sundays. Sorta milling round. Getting in each other's way. If we don't get out or stick to our rooms. See the kid up on the fence—sorta natural to talk to him."

"Did you ever see Keith Hounsell talk to him?"

"Never around. Come Friday, he'd be off into the wild blue yonder. Hunting. Fishing. Wouldn't see him again till Sunday night." His eyes sparkled. "Sundays sometimes he'd bring in a sack of crays. We'd boil them up in the copper in the yard there."

"And Tommy White?"

Thompson started. "Yeh. Tommy White. Sometimes. He'd see us getting the crays out and one, two, three, he'd be over the fence. Hounsell always gave him a couple to take home. Talked to him then maybe. Must have." He looked at Peacock, Steven, smiled knowingly. "What's this with Hounsell, eh? Got something on him?"

Peacock shook his head. "We have nothing on Mr Hounsell. But he was trying to get in touch with Tommy this morning, shortly before the boy—disappeared. Naturally, we're curious."

"Yeh, I heard that. Kept asking the kid to come down—look at his guns. Damn fool thing. But Ma White scotched that."

"So we understand. Now, Mr Thompson, one more question. You came from Turangi originally. Go back there much?"

Thompson shrugged. "Long weekends sometimes. The old lady still living there. Expects me to turn up now and then."

"Easter, for instance?"

"Sure. Easter. Why?"

"Nothing at this stage, Mr Thompson." He paused as a cadet entered with a typed message. He read it quickly, nodded. "Right. That will be all, Mr Thompson. We'll have Mr Heath next."

He waited till the door closed, turned to Steven. "Prelim report. Whittaker. Internal bruising at nape of neck, cracked vertebrae."

132

CHAPTER XV

HEATH ENTERED, charcoal grey windcheater zipped discreetly to the neck, knife edges on matching trousers. He sat precisely on the chair, balanced a soft grey hat on his knee.

"Won't keep you long, Mr Heath," said Peacock. "You've heard of Tommy White's death? We are trying to establish his movements this morning. Did you see him at all?"

"No. Don't think so."

"Your room's right opposite, isn't it?"

"Yes. But I keep the blinds drawn. Self defence, Inspector. You don't know what it's like to look up, find that kid staring at you. Gives you the willies."

"Were you home all morning?"

"No. Went into Wellington. Got back around one-thirty."

"What time did you go in?"

"Later than I'd planned. Meant to catch the ten o'clock bus. Missed it. Got the half past."

"Which stop?"

"Jackson Street. By the chemist. Didn't stay put though. Wandered around. Y'know. Boring just waiting."

"Right. You caught the ten-thirty bus into town." He made a note on the pad before him. "Now, while you're here, Mr Heath. You had an entry in the bounty competition. Identify the bandits."

Heath stiffened. "Not me, Inspector. Not my style."

"There was an entry in your name, Mr Heath."

"Oh!" He frowned. "Thompson, I bet. Asked me if I was giving it a go. But I said no show. Of course, I knew the Blaney bit. Guess everyone at Hudson House did. So most of them must've tried."

133

"Yes. Most of them did. But two entries were in the same handwriting. Yours and Thompson's."

Heath nodded. "Yeh. Typical Thompson. Do anything for a fast buck. Well, if you've finished with me——"

"Not quite, Mr Heath. Couple of points in your earlier statement. You came down here from Taupo week after Easter. Been here ever since."

"Well, a few fly trips long weekends. Business back home."

"Yes, business. I understand your business is a restaurant. Reasonably prosperous. Yet you're down here working night shift in a factory?"

"Partners only, Inspector, and, well, we're expanding. In a big way." He leaned forward confidentially. "Fact is, the owner of the building served notice he was planning to sell. Couldn't guarantee our leases after 31 July. But he did offer us first refusal. We grabbed it with both hands, raised the ante the hard way. Into hock right up to our necks. Then one of our tenants decided not to renew. An ideal place for a Dine-and-Dance restaurant. Something we've always wanted. So there we were—fresh out of the ready, and this golden opportunity staring us in the face. We tried the money people again but nobody wanted to know. And to make it worth while we simply had to be ready for the season."

He shrugged. "So what to do? We had a heavy conference. Decided one of us had to become a wage slave for a bit. Me. Because I'm the new boy, y'see. Only bought in three years ago."

"You had the job lined up before you came?"

"Too right. Puku Thompson fixed that. Came into the eatery one night talking money. I asked him what chances getting a job at Stacey's. Night shift. And he said—easy. Difficulty was finding somewhere to live but he knew there was a room at Hudson. When he got back, he put the hard word on Siggy. Fixed that, too." He grinned. "Not entirely brotherly love, y'know. Stacey's pay a $30 bonus for new staff. Easy money for Thompson."

"And have you made it, Mr Heath?"

"Made it, Inspector. Even with secondary tax. Y'see, my expenses practically nil. Taupo Restaurant pays Hudson House.

134

Stacey's take me to and from. And weekends I'm relieving cook at the Central."

"Busy man. I suppose you have a grand opening planned."

"You telling me! 1st December. A real wingding. Old Taupo won't know what hit it!" He chuckled. "Say, Inspector, any time you're our way, why don't you drop in. See how things are going."

Peacock smiled. "I might even do that, Mr Heath. Now, would you tell young Bristowe to come in?"

Bristowe was nervous. His shadowed eyes darted from Peacock to Steven, back to Peacock, as he sat on the edge of the chair, rubbing damp palms against the seams of blue jeans, too-small jacket emphasizing bony wrists, overlarge hands.

Peacock began quietly. "We won't keep you long, Alan. We just want to know what you were doing this morning."

Bristowe licked his full lips. "Nothing. Didn't do nothing."

"Puku Thompson said you were sunbathing."

"Yeh. That's it. Sunbathing." He relaxed slightly. "Don't get enough sun. Night shift, y'know."

"Yes, we know. Okay—you got up, had breakfast, went straight out to sunbathe. By the back porch out of the wind?"

"More or less. Wrote to Mum first. In my room, y'know. Then got a blanket. Coupla books. By then all the fellas gone. Day-shift jokers, y'know. So goodoh to be out there."

"Did you see Tommy White at all?"

"Tommy! No, I never saw Tommy!" The dark eyes suddenly brimmed, the voice thickened. "Poor little devil! They could've left him alone. They could've. And now he's dead! Drowned! A kid like that!"

"You liked Tommy, did you?" Peacock asked gently.

"Yeh. Nice kid. 'Course you couldn't talk to him or nothing. He wasn't, well, he wasn't—y'know. But friendly like. Follow you round like a pup. And he didn't do that Blaney job, Inspector. He didn't. Don't take no notice of what people say. He didn't do it. Couldn't have."

Peacock blinked slightly. "How d'you know?"

But Bristowe had spent his energy in that fierce denial. He collapsed back into himself, frightened perhaps by his outburst.

135

"If you gotta blame someone," he mumbled. "Blame that Hounsell fella. Shouldn'ta left guns around so's a kid like that could get hold of them."

Peacock sighed. "Did you hear Hounsell calling Tommy?"

"Yeh. Didn't take any notice but. Reading, y'know," he added with an air of triumph. Steven speculated fleetingly on what particular book, decided not to ask. It was not important.

"You didn't see Hounsell?"

"No. Didn't see anyone."

"Except Puku Thompson?"

"Yeh. Puku. Came and sat on the porch."

"Then he went up town for lunch. Did you go, too?"

"No," Bristowe wriggled slightly. "Bit short. Just enough coupla meals. Pay day to-morrow, y'know."

"Would you know what time Thompson left?"

"Dunno. After the ten o'clock whistle, that's all."

"And you stayed in the sun till——?"

"Waited for the twelve o'clock. Then I went inside. Tried to get a bit of kip. Y'know, I gotta work all night."

"Well, we'll leave it at that, Alan. There's a car waiting to take you and the others so you won't be late."

Peacock waved dismissal, Bristowe jumped up, face illuminated with a relieved grin, flashed out of the door.

"Thought we had something there, for a while," commented Peacock. "The only one who admits chatting with Tommy."

He selected the chart prepared after Blaney's death, carefully placed a tick alongside Bristowe's name under the heading "Can talk to Tommy". There were only four other names so ticked—Collins, Cumming, Dr and Mrs White.

"Interesting to know what Bristowe spends his money on," mused Steven. "Living from pay day to pay day like that."

Peacock spoke crisply. "He's on probation, remember. Probably part of his pay is banked at source."

Steven nodded, bent to examine the chart. He pointed to the column headed "Knew about the gun". "You're guessing a bit there. Hounsell's really the only one."

"Educated guess. Cumming because Tommy could've told him. Likewise the Whites. Wilkins, well, possible, eh?"

They looked up as a cadet entered. He handed more papers to Steven, spoke to Peacock. "Excuse me, sir, but Inspector Blaney would like a word with you. If it's convenient."

"Of course. Bring him in. Bring him in." Peacock went to the door, escorted the waiting man into the room. "Understand you were on the search to-day?"

"Yes. Felt better doing something." An older Joe Blaney, thinner, eyes surprisingly calm.

"Fairbrother been keeping you informed?" asked Peacock and, at the other's nod, continued. "Thing that's throwing us is lack of motive. We can't find any reason. None at all."

"No. Stumped me, too. Could be because he's police."

"I hope not. Joe told you about the Collins case?"

"Some. No names, the bare outline. Brian Fairbrother filled me in when I came down. I asked him about it."

"Joe thought he had it licked. Did he mention that?"

"Yes. Last letter he wrote. Had to wait till Collins was on nights. To prove it, I mean."

"He didn't give you any hint about how he planned to obtain this proof?"

"No. But he'd really hit on something, I think. Wanted to keep it to himself till he'd tried it out."

"You were pleased about that?"

"Naturally. Especially as he was so enthusiastic."

Peacock frowned. There was a slight nuance in the voice which defied interpretation. "Joe was doing very well in the force," he said carefully. "At least, as far as can be gathered from reports. How did he feel about it—inside?"

"He was thinking of resigning," Blaney said reluctantly. "I was hoping this Collins thing would change that. That's why— well, I did build it up a bit. Maybe that's why he kept it to himself. Now, no one knows what he had in mind."

"He kept it to himself because those were his instructions. Police involvement, remember. Fairbrother didn't see any point in swapping one name for another. No proof, no names. And someone else does know. Lance Brendon."

Blaney brightened. "Then you know all about it?"

Peacock smiled wryly. "Not yet. Fairbrother's instructions apply to Brendon, too. He's made that quite clear."

Blaney looked thoughtful. "Yes. Sounds like Brian."

"Well, getting back to Joe. You said he was thinking of leaving the force. There was a reason?"

"Nothing specific. Just a bit of bad luck lately, that's all. Twice in hospital this year."

"That's right. We've had abridged reports of the incidents. Napier assault—concussion. Eight stitches, three days in hospital. Taupo car accident—broken ribs, bone in right foot, minor internal, month in hospital. End February. Beginning of April. That's the reason?"

"Yes. One on top of the other. Nearly bought it the second time. They reckon if he'd pulled right instead of left, he'd have gone over the cliff."

"Luck," said Peacock. "Or extremely good driving."

Blaney nodded, eyes lowered, face tight, carefully emptied of expression.

"So now we come to Tommy White's murder." The harshly-spoken words had the desired effect. Blaney's head jerked up, eyes narrowed, alert.

"You know definitely?" he queried.

"It was murder. But we're just starting on this one. Maybe it'll give us the lead we want."

Blaney hesitated, recognizing the signs of dismissal. "Better let you get on with it then. Thanks for filling me in."

He paused in the doorway. "I was hoping——Going back on Thursday. D'you think——"

"Anything we find out, you will be the first to know."

Blaney nodded, let himself out of the room. Steven looked at Peacock but the older man did not move. He was staring at the door as though something had struck him, something he was trying to pin down. At last he sighed. "Ever been knocked around in the line of duty?" he asked abruptly.

"Yes," said Steven without elaborating. His fingers strayed to the faint scar under his left eye, a reminder of his first encounter with viciousness. Three weeks out of training, he had

138

been assisting in breaking up a hotel fracas when his own arrestee smashed a glass against the bar, plunged the jagged shards into his face.

"How did you feel about it?"

"I felt like quitting." That had been later when he realized how close he had come to losing an eye.

Peacock looked at him vaguely. "Yes. I guess we all feel that way some time or other. Anything new?" He indicated the pile of papers in front of Steven.

"Yes. Hounsell's been cleared. Remember you said Hounsell wouldn't use his own car. A Land Rover would be a bit too conspicuous. Well, Palmerston started checking out the hire car people then gave it away when Thomas reported in."

"Thomas?"

"The man sent up to Massey to interview Professor Hounsell."

Steven nodded. "Yes, he confirmed Keith was with him from five to six, happened to mention he knew he was coming because the office had warned him. So Thomas went along to check on that and it seems Hounsell called in around two-thirty. To find out when his brother would be free.

"Sooooo. That lets Hounsell out. He couldn't be in Petone at two and Palmerston at half past. And this morning——" He shifted to a more comfortable position. "This morning he spent most of the time filling those bottles and swapping yarns with the chap in the Underwater shop. What about the others? Any reports yet?"

"Preliminary reports. Six on Hudson House people. All clear because it's a work day. Brendon on duty, also. Arline Muir. Gregg was at this meeting of the career officers Union."

"Yes. Gregg—his background. Young Brendon, maybe. But Blaney? Nothing there. Mrs Gregg wasn't interested in Blaney."

"Blaney could've been interested in Gregg."

"Yes. Could be." Steven waited while Peacock thought about that. Some interesting facts had emerged in the routine investigation into Gregg's background.

After fifteen years with the bank, he had resigned to go into business for himself, failed dismally, crawled back into a minor

139

position with his former employer. Add an extravagant, thoughtless wife and there were ingredients for police interest. Maybe Blaney had stumbled on to something, maybe . . .

Judging correctly when to interrupt Peacock's reflections, Steven continued. "Collins was asleep. Desk rang Mrs Collins about Tommy at one-fifteen. She said she wouldn't wake him but she must have because Collins flagged down one of the cars later. Out searching in the western hills area."

Peacock nodded. "Ever met Mrs Collins? Fine woman. Never forgiven us for being even slightly suspicious of her dear Harvey. So Collins was asleep, eh? Been on nights twice now, hasn't he? Nothing's happened?"

"Nothing's happened," agreed Steven, brushing aside the obvious detour. "And unless something turns up soon, nothing here either. Only thing we've got is someone looking like a policeman on the other side of the road."

"Yes, a man in a blue shirt. But we need another sighting. Still, it follows. Have to keep tabs on Tommy. Make sure he went to the stopbank. So he'd be close by. How long would it take Tommy to get there? Ten minutes? Fifteen?"

"Thereabouts. Provided he wasn't diverted. The way Tommy lopes along. Covers the ground like nobody's business."

"Well, he was on Emerson Street at ten-three so the stopbank ten past, quarter past. How soon after that did he die?"

"Five minutes. If Blue Shirt's our man."

"So the earliest—perhaps ten-twenty. Doc said six to eight hours. Which would make his earliest quarter to eleven. Near enough, I suppose."

"And if Blue Shirt is not our man?"

"Well, any time up to quarter to one. But you don't really believe that, do you?"

"Maybe not. But someone could've met Tommy wandering around. Suggested the stopbank."

"Could be. Maybe house to house will turn up something. But don't forget, Tommy was carrying this yacht. That looks like purpose. No other still water in that direction, is there?"

"Not to my knowledge. One of the locals would know."

"Ask them. Then we have to decide why Tommy was killed."

140

Steven looked up sharply. "Obvious, isn't it? Tommy could identify him."

"But he wasn't worried about that at the start, was he? Handed Tommy to us on a platter."

"Well, he'd be safer with Tommy out of the way. Must've thought about it."

"And left it till Monday? Too much of a risk. Friday, Saturday even. But Monday? No, something happened to make Tommy a potential danger."

"We decided Tommy didn't kill Blaney?"

Peacock grimaced, said doubtfully, "Perhaps. But I can't help feeling there's something else. Something we haven't realized the significance . . ." His voice trailed into silence. Presently he shrugged. "No. Maybe you're right. Maybe that's all it was."

CHAPTER XVI

STEVEN SHOVED THE chart away in disgust. He was pushing too much, trying to make sense out of insufficient information.

"Don't like it?" asked Peacock looking up from his notes.

"Don't like any of it. Nothing fits. Nobody had a reason——" He laughed ruefully. "Had White lined up there once. Well, he was missing between ten and eleven. Claims he was in the library sketching costumes for this new production. Maybe he was but the librarian didn't see him go in. Can't prove he was there all the time."

"That's a point. And the motive?"

"Well, he believed Tommy killed Blaney. He could see what's coming. Arrest. Trial. Commitment. What have you. This way quicker. Less anguish for Mrs White."

"Deadlier, too. You've seen Mrs White. And don't forget White's seen her in shock once before." He smiled grimly. "Y'see, I've already travelled that path. Even tried to fit him in with Blaney's death. Why not? Tech. so handy. Only a few minutes walk. But, those ministry officials arrived at one-forty-five, were with him till four. Look, we've both missed a meal. There's a fish-and-chip shop just around the corner in Jackson Street. How about getting me a dozen oysters and ten cents chips."

Steven collected the money, grateful for a chance to go out into the fresh air. The night was crisp and clear. The day's heat had succumbed to a cold sea breeze, laden with the salty water-talk of the incoming tide.

Steven walked along Elizabeth Street, entered Jackson Street, deserted at the mid-evening hour, lit by spaced street lights,

142

random swathes of subdued lighting from shop windows.

He was about to enter the fish shop when a car pulled into the kerb, a voice hailed him. He turned to find Lance Brendon stretched across the seat of his ancient car busily winding down the window.

Steven crossed the pavement, leaned against the door. "Hi, there. All on your lonesome?"

"You're so right. Did you expect something different?"

"Sure! Night off! Thought you'd be out with one of your floosies."

Brendon giggled. "Too busy for females. Get in, will you. Want to talk to you."

Steven climbed aboard. "Wanted to see you myself. Couple of questions. For instance, d'you know if Joe ever went to Hudson House? To play cards or suchlike?"

Brendon pursed his lips. "Not to my knowledge. 'Course I asked him. When he first came. But he thought cards a waste of time."

"But you went fairly regularly."

"Why, sure. Not a crime, is it? Say, what's this? An inquisition? I thought I was in the clear. Like—I was doing escort duty when young Tommy was done in."

"The official version is drowned," said Steven quietly.

"Drowned, my foot. Use your loaf, man. Tommy was a danger to whoever—and he drowns! It just happened that way! Come on!"

"Nevertheless we have to keep an open mind. We can't overlook the fact that it may be just a coincidence."

Brendon drew in a sharp breath. "So that's it, is it? Oh, I know how you law boys think. Like—I was the last one to see Joe alive. Like—I arranged for the street to be empty. I suppose old Pruneface——"

He stopped in mid-sentence as the sound of the fire siren sliced the night. "A fire," he whispered. "By all that's holy, a fire! Let's hope it's a good one."

He swung round, gazed at the warning lights at the Buick Street intersection. Steven watched him curiously, puzzled by the expectant attitude, the exultant glow in his face.

143

With the first sound of the siren, the empty street erupted into life. Cars converged on the fire station, a man in fireman's uniform went past on a bicycle, pedalling furiously, a black traffic car swooped across the main street, paused momentarily in the red glare of the flashing lights, zoomed onwards.

"That'll be Rex—Rex Dunstan," said Brendon. "He's on local control to-night."

"Picked Collins up when he stopped then, did he?"

"Could be. He was up that way. Going towards Cuba Street."

They listened as the first engine screamed away, gauged the location of the fire. Brendon leaned out of the car, looked eastwards, gave an excited whoop. "There she is. Look! Down on the beach. One of those factories. Let's hope it's a good one——"

Steven felt uneasy. Brendon was displaying all the symptoms of a firebug. He sat there in an aura of suppressed excitement, counting the engines as they made their way to where the flames were painting the sky with hazy menace.

"Listen," said Brendon. Far to the north came the sound of a fire engine speeding south. "It's a big one. That'll be Lower Hutt sending reinforcements."

He leaned forward to start the engine.

"Hey, wait a minute," cried Steven, groping for the door. "I'm supposed to be getting Jonas some chish."

"Skip it. You've got more important things to do." Brendon hesitated, looked at Steven. "Aren't you coming?" he asked.

"Coming?" repeated Steven, puzzled by the disappointed tone. Then it penetrated. Brendon had said Monday to Wednesday, had stipulated a happening, so the fire—— "Of course, I'm coming".

Brendon gave a relieved grin, swung the car around, sped westwards towards the railway station, rounded the traffic island, cruised slowly back the length of Jackson Street. At Cuba Street, the virtual end of the shopping area, he stopped the car around the corner, sat for five finger-tapping minutes watching the distant glow.

"Now," he said grimly as he swung the car almost savagely back into Jackson Street. "If he doesn't show this time——"

Steven frowned, eyes intent on the empty road, the empty pavements. After the sudden flurry caused by the fire, the town had lapsed back into somnolence.

They were approaching the post office when Steven straightened, stared ahead at a policeman going through the routine of checking doors.

"There! South side! Just by the chemist!"

Brendon nodded, turned leisurely at the post office corner, cruised halfway down the side street, into another cross street, parked the car. They ran back to the corner, looked towards Jackson Street.

"Over there," said Brendon, pointing to the gateway marking the post office yard. "Plenty of shadow. Quiet, now!"

They ran lightly across the narrow road, settled into the concealing darkness of the gateway. It was a good position. They could see the other side of Jackson Street and the uniform man checking the doors of the library on the corner of Bay Street.

"Didn't think he'd strike before," whispered Brendon. "Only the toy shop, council offices and now the library."

"Seems to be taking a good look at Bay Street."

"Checking to see if anyone's around—like."

The man left the library, crossed the intersection, stepped on to the pavement, looked up and down the main street, moved over to the estate agent's office, checked the door, moved into the recessed doorway of Barne Evan's Electrical—and stayed there.

After a few minutes, Brendon nodded. "Well, that's it. Barne Evan's Electrical."

Steven hesitated. From this angle they could not see the actual entrance. The soft light from the window display spilled gently on to the pavement throwing the rear area into shadow.

The man could still be there, motionless, waiting, or he could have gone into the shop as they believed. Steven was about to voice his doubts to Brendon when a stray car swooshed by, flooding the empty doorway with light.

"Yes, that's it," said Steven grimly. "Better get on the other side so we can get him when he comes out."

145

Brendon straightened. "Should be all right if we wander along now. Like—we've just made the scene, eh?"

They walked along to Jackson Street, two late-night pedestrians out for an evening stroll. They crossed over to Clary's, stepped into the mosaic-tiled foyer. Facing the large window, they gazed absently at the brightly lit display.

"He'll come this way," said Brendon. "Keep up the show a bit then fade out. That's the way Joe reckoned. So far it's gone right all along the line."

"Maybe. But you know what's happening. I don't."

Brendon smiled at Steven's testiness. "Take it easy, chum. I'll deal you in. You know about this Collins inquiry?"

"Yes."

"Well, they dumped this thing on to Joe. All the evidence to date, conclusions, the lot. Nothing proved. Joe waded through it all. Got bogged down like the rest. Thought he was swotting for sergeant's exam or something. The time he spent on it. Like I said, he was getting nowhere fast. Almost gave it away then one night——"

He shook his head in wonder. "Y'know, that's exactly how it happened. Joe asked me one night what I thought of a guy who went to the bother of pinching a box of hinges."

"A box of hinges!" repeated Steven incredulously.

"Yeh. Part of the loot from Tolley's. I said the guy's nuts. Straight away. And Joe said, 'Yes, maybe that's it. Got a kink somewhere anyway.' That's when I got dragged into it. Not dragged exactly. Stood on Joe to get a bit of the action. Well, first we looked at this crazy loot thing. Four times it happened. Like—gemstones instead of diamonds. Like—plastic instead of silver. And pocket torches instead of pocket transistors."

"Easier to get at maybe?"

"You reckon? Right beside the pricier stuff in every case. So why not take the pricier stuff. And here's another odd thing. Never took too much any time. Biggest job worth about $500. Watches and gemstones. Why not all watches? Diamonds?"

"Easier to sell?"

"Sell!" Brendon snorted. "Guy doesn't sell the stuff. Nothing's shown, y'know, but nothing. No place. Not one item. Like it

146

was planted somewhere. Like the guy wasn't interested in unloading it."

"Then why steal in the first place?"

"You tell me. I told you it didn't make sense. Nothing about this crazy case does. And get a load of this. Everything taken from somewhere obvious. Window display. Inside display stand. So the shoppie noticed as soon as he opened up."

"He wanted it to be noticed."

"Looked like. Which was odd, to say the least. But there were plenty of odd things. Like—only when Collins was on. Only when there was a fire. No signs of breaking and entering. And always small stuff, stuff you could cart away in your pocket like. So we started looking at the non-things."

"The non-things?" Steven frowned, looked sharply at Brendon but the traffic officer was deadly serious.

"Yes, the things that weren't. We'd looked at the facts. Got no place. So why not look at the non-facts. Follows. Like—who wasn't on duty the nights of the burglaries. Who wasn't on the Petone force. Who wasn't married."

Steven was completely out of his depth but he presumed it made sense to Brendon.

"Well, it sifted down to five men. We checked their rosters again and, lo and behold!—one man was on duty twice when there was a fire on Collins' shift but no burglaries."

"That was suspicious?"

"To us it was. Y'see, when he's on duty he's out of Petone. When he's off duty, he's right here. Lives here."

So it was as simple as that. It sounded straightforward, direct, but Steven could guess how many man hours would be involved in painstakingly sifting through night rosters over eighteen months then retracking to look at the ones not on duty.

"I didn't know he lived here," said Steven quietly.

He had recognized the man as he paused under the street light—Gordon Stroud, attached to the Lower Hutt force. Well, it had to be police, no matter how much the thought nauseated, but Gordon Stroud!

Steven knew him superficially, a face amongst a hundred other faces, a quiet nothing who landed all the kidstuff, the natural butt of the bright boys, those same bright boys he had kept jumping for eighteen months without detection. He must have been laughing himself sick every time he pulled off one of his mysterious burglaries.

"Everything fits, does it?"

"Everything. Used to be on the Petone force. Transferred to Lower Hutt two months before the first strike. Knows the area well, shopkeepers, so on. Could be planned it then. Helped himself to keys, patterns of keys. Always off duty when a break occurred. Lives two doors away from Collins so probably knew when Collins was on nights. And he's separated. Wife left couple of years ago."

"D'you know why?"

"Nope. But no matter. Means he's living alone. No one to notice when he went out. What he brought home."

"Why didn't you tell Fairbrother?"

"No names till proven, he said. We had to wait."

"Did Blaney arrange for Collins to do nights last month?"

"Yeh. Told Fairbrother nothing would happen. And it didn't. This week different. Stroud was off duty."

He paused, sidled over to the edge of the foyer, peered towards Barne Evan's Electrical, moved back. "Not yet. Won't be long now. Never stays too long in one place as far as Joe could figure."

"Where was he Friday afternoon?" Steven asked flatly.

Brendon shook his head. "Nothing doing. On duty at the court. I checked. First thing I did." He stood squarely in front of Steven. "Well?" he asked.

"Yes. I'm convinced. We'll pick him up."

Brendon made another check, nodded. "Yes, I like that one," he said in a normal voice. "Suit Kylie down to the ground. Come along, we're running a bit late."

They walked out on to the pavement as though they had merely paused to look at the window display. Stroud, who had been walking towards them, turned into the entrance of a menswear shop.

"Night, officer," said Brendon cheekily.

"Night," came the gruff reply, head averted as though interested in the contents of the window.

Steven turned into the doorway. "Evening, Stroud," he said quietly. "Wasn't expecting to see you to-night."

Stroud swung round to face him. "Evening, sir. Doing a bit of window shopping. Got a couple of birthdays coming up."

Steven examined the man's face closely. He seemed relaxed, unperturbed, complacent almost. Steven had expected wariness, nothing like this chatty comment on the merits of a cardigan on display.

Surely the man realized he would be under suspicion as soon as the robbery was reported. Then Steven knew with sudden clarity that, if he took no action, walked away as though from a casual meeting, there would be no burglary reported to-morrow.

Stroud would realize his danger, rectify it. If he could enter the shop to steal, he could as easily enter to replace the goods he had taken, a simple expedient to protect himself.

No wonder he was unconcerned, thoroughly at ease. There was nothing to show he had been pilfering. His hands were empty. The pockets of his tunic lay flat. If Steven had not actually seen the evidence of the empty doorway, he would have been reluctant to act.

Even so he felt a moment of doubt. The man so obviously had nothing on him. Maybe this time he had decided against taking anything. He stood there, round-faced, benign, slightly rotund, paunchy. A mental picture of Stroud standing on the edge of the pavement looking up and down the street leaped into Steven's mind. Not so rotund, not so paunchy.

"You're under arrest, Stroud," he said firmly. "For complicity in several cases of burglary over the last two years."

He nodded to Brendon, hovering expectantly, and the transport man galloped off to fetch his car.

Stroud looked at the retreating form, back at Steven, shook a puzzled head. "You're making a mistake, sir. A grave error." His manner was fatherly, an older officer who knew the system anxious to save a youngster from the follies of over eagerness. "I know the cases you refer to. And the talk of a policeman in the vicinity. But you're beating the gun, sir. Very dangerous, if I may say so. There hasn't been a burglary in months——"

149

Steven broke in wearily. "That's quite correct. But there was one to-night, wasn't there, Stroud? We've been watching you for the last half hour. We know you went into Barne Evan's Electrical."

CHAPTER XVII

SENIOR CONSTABLE MOORHEAD spread the articles on the small table, rearranged the pattern, shook his head.

"Hardly an intelligent selection," he commented. He did not look at Stroud. In fact, no one seemed to be looking at Stroud. He stood apart, ignored.

Steven agreed with Moorhead. Crazy loot. Three electric razors, two pocket transistors, six paua shell ashtrays, four sets of stainless-steel serviette rings. Serviette rings, for heaven's sake!

He lifted the waistcoat Stroud had been wearing under his jacket, heavy nylon canvas with a dozen pockets on the inside.

"Busy, Sergeant? Or just filling in time?" Peacock's sarcastic voice behind him made Steven jump guiltily but he was saved by the irrepressible Brendon.

"We nailed him, Inspector. Just like Joe said. Collins went down to the fire so we kept a dekko on things and this cove——" He jerked a thumb at the indifferent Stroud. "He raided Barne Evan's Electrical."

Peacock's heavy frown lifted. He moved over to the table, fingered the ashtrays. "Hardly raided. Not even enterprising. Good work, Brendon. You ought to join the force."

He turned to Stroud. "You!" he barked. "I want to talk to you. Go into the office. And you!" He turned to Steven. "Fetch Collins in. The sooner he knows about this the better."

Steven ran out to the car, was starting the engine when Brendon scrambled into the passenger seat. "Might as well be in on the kill," he commented smugly.

Steven grinned, turned the car towards the beach. "Fire's

151

kaput, by the look of things. That's something anyway."

Only one fire engine was operating when they stopped at the fringe of the thinning crowd, close to where Collins stood.

Steven slid out of the car, walked over to the uniform man. "Everything under control?" he asked.

Collins glanced at him briefly. "Yes. A good save. Two more hours then standby."

"Good. Then it won't matter if you leave it to Rex. You're wanted back at the station."

Collins stiffened. "Another one?" he asked bitterly.

"Another one," agreed Steven. "But we caught him this time, Collins. Inspector Peacock wanted you to know as soon as possible. Coming?"

"I'm coming," relief lifting his voice. "Sure I'm coming."

He did not seem surprised to find Brendon in the car, squeezed in beside him at the transport man's insistence.

"I suppose I owe this to Cocky," he said when they were under way.

"No," said Steven, guessing Cocky would be Peacock's probationary nickname. "Joe Blaney's the one. And Lance here. Jonas had nothing to do with it."

"Joe Blaney? What was he——?" He stopped, realizing it was a logical step. "Someone I know?" he asked diffidently.

"Someone you know. Had to be."

Collins was silent, almost gloomy until Brendon started light-heartedly outlining the inquiry. When they arrived back, spilled out on to the steps, Brendon grabbed Collins' hand, pumped it up and down.

"Good luck, Harve. Everything's going your way now."

"You leaving?" Collins asked, puzzled.

"Sure I'm leaving. Be in the way. Those law boys will be having a heyday. Swarming all over you. Besides," he put on a knowing leer, "Gig Forest's wetting the baby's head to-night. Might be in time for a noggin if I get cracking."

He dashed over to his car, climbed aboard, waved as they went up the steps into the welcome he had predicted.

They were still milling around Collins in a congratulatory amoeba when Peacock came out of the front office, the crestfallen Stroud trailing behind. "All right. He's ready to make a statement. Anyone want to take him on?"

Steven watched Collins, saw the blank astonishment on his face. Collins strode over to Stroud. "Gordon! You! Why?"

But Stroud had had enough. He averted his eyes, followed a reluctant constable to another room.

"Come in here," said Jonas. "I'll spell it out for you." As Steven drew level, Jonas held out his hand, demanded, "Well?"

"Sorry, sir. Forgot all about it." Hurriedly, Steven pulled out the coins, passed them over. "Got tied up with this Stroud thing," he added hopefully.

Jonas grunted, jerked his head to where Collins was waiting self-consciously, followed Steven into the room, closed the door.

"Sit down. Sit down," he said briskly and when Collins was sitting there with a disbelieving frown on his face, he added almost kindly, "He hated you, y'know".

Collins flushed, mumbled, "Yes. That must be it. Must be."

"Ever had a showdown with him?"

"Well, yes, once. He—we—well, there was nearly a mix-in. But I thought he'd got over that. A couple of years ago."

Jason nodded. "That'd be just before his wife left him?"

"Yes, but that wasn't why—— I mean, Louise didn't leave him because of me or anything like that."

"Oh, I wouldn't say that. I'd say you were the principal reason all right. Not that you could've done anything to prevent it." He talked softly, officially. "You're a good officer, Collins. Excellent record. Stroud's wife knew that. Kept telling him how good you were, how well-liked. Sniping at him because he wasn't within cooey. It got on his nerves. That's why he blew that time. But that wasn't why she left him. That happened after the Gohlen case. Right?"

"That would be about it. I remember Louise, well, she took it pretty badly when he landed that reprimand."

"Unfortunately for you. But he deserved it. Made a real mess of that one. Overzealous maybe, but stupid also. Probably anxious to show everyone he was as good as you. Anyway,

153

after that, she told him he was a no-hoper and cleared out."

Collins considered slowly, nodded. "Yes, that way I guess I caused it all right. But he'd have to be sick to blame me, just the same."

"He's sick. Thinks you're the cause of all his misfortunes. That's why he wanted to break you. Nearly succeeded, too. Got you suspended anyway. Then when you were re-instated he couldn't take it. Made him all the more determined. And he knew just how to do it. One more burglary and——" He flicked his hand.

Collins' mouth twisted wryly. "Y'know, he used to come round when I was suspended. All sympathy. Said it was enough to make a fellow resign. I thought he meant it. And all the time, all the time he must've been gloating."

"No doubt. Luckily you didn't take his advice and resign. Would've played right into his hands." He paused as a constable entered.

"Report from the men who went round to Stroud's, sir. Stuff's all there. Three suitcases in a back bedroom."

He withdrew as Peacock stood up, moved around the table, clapped Collins on the shoulder. "Well, there it is, Collie. All cleared up. You're home and dry. And I think the best thing for you to do right now is go home and tell Myra, eh?"

"Yes, of course. And thanks, Jonas. Thanks." Collins stood a moment blinking uncertainly, then turned quickly, closed the door quietly behind him.

Peacock sat down at the desk. "Glad about that," he said gruffly. "Old Collie's a good bloke."

"You didn't have too much trouble with Stroud, I gather," said Steven.

"No trouble," said Peacock airily. "Just talked about how easily an innocent man could be made to look guilty then drifted on to the Blaney case. Happened to mention it looked as though the two cases had a connection. Soon as Stroud jerried to what I was getting at he couldn't get out from under fast enough. Spilled out of him. Bottled up so long someone had to catch the flood. And I was the one."

"He was at the court at the time of the shooting."

154

"Yes. So I understand. And if he'd been thinking straight he'd have known it was so much hogwash. But he was so scared of being involved he thought admitting to the Collins deal seemed the easier way out." He consulted a piece of paper on his desk. "Well, I think we'll call it a day. To-morrow first thing we'll be going into Wellington. Kelvin Chambers. I have an appointment at nine."

But the day began earlier than that. At seven-thirty they were back on High Street. Arline Muir had agreed to see Jonas as long as he realized she had to catch the eight o'clock bus.

As they climbed the narrow stairs, Steven hoped the girls had enough warning to be ready for visitors. He need not have worried. When they knocked on the bright orange door, it was opened sharply by an almost-hostile Arline, dressed for the street.

"Oh, it's you. Come in. But remember, I haven't too much time. You'll have to put up with my moving around—y'know."

She led the way to the kitchen where she finished wiping dishes, putting them away in a cupboard over the sink.

"Miss Clark home?" asked Peacock.

"Not yet. She's a nurse, y'know. On night shift. Home about eight-fifteen." She held up the tea towel she had been using, decided it was in need of a wash, flung it into the plastic clothes basket in the corner.

"If it's Judy you want to see, why didn't you say——"

"No, it's you, Miss Muir. We want to talk about Joe Blaney."

Arline shrugged, went into the living-room, began to move cushions into more striking patterns. Peacock lifted an eyebrow at Steven, followed.

"Miss Muir. Think carefully, will you? Did Joe ever tell you he thought someone was after him? Anything like that?"

Arline looked straight at him, sneered openly. "You've already asked me that. Don't you remember what I said or are you trying to trap me?"

"We're trying to find the truth, Miss Muir," said Peacock patiently.

155

Arline swung away, stood looking out of the window. When she turned, her lips were tight. "I told you Joe had been attacked. You——" She tossed her head in Steven's direction. "You said it was an accident. Accident! No way! That fellow left the car slung right across the road. Deliberately. Joe couldn't help ploughing right into it."

"Right, Miss Muir. We'll concede it was a deliberate effort to obstruct the police, yes. But Joe Blaney in particular? This man was trying to escape. The fact that the pursuing car was driven by Blaney, that he might be hurt, was quite incidental."

"Quite incidental! My, my! Aren't we polite. The dear little criminal is innocent until he's proved guilty, is that it? How can you be so godalmighty sure when you don't even know who was responsible?"

Arline stood in front of them, hands clenching and unclenching, lips thin, etched with tight white lines, eyes wide with frustrated rage. Yet Steven sensed it was not wholly caused by the apparent thick-headedness of the police. She had been steamily angry even before they had arrived, was using them as an outlet for her pent-up emotions.

Peacock made no comment. He knew from experience how silence could turn anger into revelation.

"And what about Napier?" she flung at them. "He was attacked there! If it hadn't been for John Citizen coming along when he did, it might've been curtains for him then, too."

"Another man trying to escape, Miss Muir. Knocked him out."

"Knocked him out! My God! What do we have to do to make you see straight?" Contempt and bitterness flooded her face, words seethed out of her. "Joe was just like you. Brainwashed. All in the line of duty, he said. But if you'd only use your bloody brains, Joe would probably be alive to-day."

She stooped to pick up her purse and gloves from the couch. "Now, if you don't mind, I have to go. We have an extraction at eight-thirty and it's my job to make the woman comfortable. Not all of us can ride around in big cars looking important. Some of us really do a job of work."

She stormed out into the tiny hall, flung open the orange

156

door, waited till the two men filed quietly out on to the small landing, slammed the door shut, checked it, swept down the stairs without a backward glance.

Steven and Peacock followed at a more leisurely pace. By the time they reached the footpath, Arline was well on her way down the street. Peacock gazed thoughtfully after her retreating form. "Wonder what that was all about. Something upset her before we arrived, I'd say. She was all right when I 'phoned earlier."

"Not now," said Steven. "And if she doesn't calm down soon she won't be much good to her patient either."

"Hello," said a voice behind them. "You're on the job early."

They turned to find Lance Brendon, a lopsided grin on his face. Peacock looked at him reflectively.

"You'd been at her first, had you?"

"Not exactly. Went up to see if Judy was home. But Arline seemed to think I should've been around last night to hold her hand or something. 'Fraid I'm not up on these things." He laughed, man to man, stopped quickly when he saw the expression on Peacock's face. "Sorry, did I muck things up for you?"

Steven shot a look at Peacock, noticed the frost, said hurriedly, "A bit. She'd have torn us to pieces, given half a chance."

"Brendon," said Peacock. "Did Joe Blaney ever tell you he thought his life was in danger?"

Brendon cocked his head on one side. "Nope. Never. Why? Has Arline been pitching you a tale again?"

Peacock grimaced. "Miss Muir was upset. But sometimes we say things in anger that normally we pretend are impossible. You supposed to be on duty?" he asked pointedly.

Brendon was not the least abashed. He indicated the patrol car parked on the other side of the street, gave a snappy salute, ran over, climbed aboard.

"That young man's too big for his britches," growled Peacock. "Come along. We haven't got all day."

The grey police car drew away from the kerb, Steven forcing himself to gentle the accelerator when all the time he wanted to slam it to the floorboards, scream through the startled traffic. He was furious with Brendon.

Last night the traffic officer had shown the better side of himself: intelligent, steadfast, sparing no effort to prove Joe Blaney's theory. Now he was playing silly devils again.

Any time now Jonas would launch into a lecture on 'When I was young and joined the force'—but oddly enough the older man remained silent, preoccupied. He did not speak until they were tooling along the motorway.

"Funny that Muir said that. About someone being after Joe."

"Because that's the way you're thinking?"

"Need to. We're not turning up anything useful in Petone. Maybe we're looking in the wrong place. Maybe something happened before he came to Petone. Besides, Inspector Blaney says Joe was thinking of resigning."

"Don't blame him either. Two near misses a mite too close for comfort."

"And if they're connected? It would explain quite a bit, wouldn't it? Why we can't find any rhyme or reason. Why nothing fits. In actual fact, the only thing we do know for certain is that the murderer was in Petone between one and two Friday, and yesterday morning between ten and twelve. Now, if we could prove he was in Taupo Easter and Napier—end of February, wasn't it?"

"Yes. Sunday 26th. We could always ask. Might even catch someone out in a lie."

"Exactly. So while you're waiting for me, you can send a flyer to Napier and Taupo. Probably have the info. on hand by the time we get back to Petone."

"How specific should I be?"

"Well, a general inquiry at this stage. Just list the names, ask if known. The Hudson House blokes—Sigley, Hounsell, Bristowe, Heath and Thompson. Then there is White—and Cumming. And for good measure what about Brendon, Collins and Wilkins."

"The Ponderosa Committee?"

"Nooo. Can't tie them in with the gun. Or Tommy White.

158

Not yet! But if we don't strike paydirt first time round, we may even drag them in later."

"We'll have to have another look at those reports."

"Yes. First thing when we get back. Go over them with a fine tooth comb. Look at them as potential murder attempts. And refer back anything not completely explained."

CHAPTER XVIII

P E A C O C K B O U N C E D I N T O the car, grinned broadly as he said, "Home, James. And don't spare the horses."

Steven glanced at him sideways. The old boy was pleased about something. Probably some hunch was working out well.

"First thing we do," said Peacock as they were once more headed towards Petone, "make an appointment to see Mrs White. I think that lady can help us. Maybe we can help her."

"I thought the first thing was a look at those incidents," said Steven drily.

"That, too, of course. You get those flyers away?"

"I did. Routed them through Lower Hutt. Thought it might save a bit of heartburn. I mean, the Petone men on the list."

Peacock laughed. "Very thoughtful of you, Sergeant. Y'know, to-day I think we're going to break this case."

But when they arrived back at the office, had time to study the reports again, they found the prosaic language had reduced both incidents to routine inquiries.

Peacock sighed heavily. "We're reaching, laddie. Really reaching. Still, one or two points of interest. Those wood-yard fires, for instance."

"Four inside eleven weeks. The first three of doubtful origin but nothing proven. The last one, definitely arson."

"Yes. Definitely arson. Why? Did he change his MO or did someone else set that last fire? Possible. For the purpose of the exercise, shall we say someone else, eh? Makes that smashed globe more significant."

"Could be. Light supposed to be on from sunset to sunrise. A pretty dark alley, by the sounds of it, and Joe had to go down there to check the side gate."

"Right. The globe was smashed when? Doesn't say. They suggest vandals but—— Blaney's mate did the one o'clock. Craddock, isn't it. John Craddock. Better contact him about that."

"Check. Y'know, Blaney was lucky. Very lucky. If he hadn't let out that yell when the torch was knocked out of his hand . . . And if Menton hadn't been close enough to hear . . . Well, it might've been a different story."

"We'll have to talk to Menton again, I think."

Menton had been strolling along the path by Torson's Woodyard when he heard Joe's startled cry. He ran to the alley, saw what was happening. Straight away he began yelling himself, making out there were others with him, charged in to help. The assailant took off down the alley, jumped a low fence at the end. Menton did not give chase, being more concerned with the injured man lying on the ground.

"No description," muttered Jonas. "A tall dark shadow running down the alley. That's all."

"More than we have for Taupo, though. In fact, Taupo—I don't know. The more I look at it, the more it looks like an accident."

"Whose side are you on? We said we'd tackle both incidents as murder attempts."

"Yes, but Taupo! I mean, Easter and all that. Place crawling with tourists. Fishermen. Car theft's sort of second nature."

"That's it! That's his MO. Makes use of what's going on wherever. Napier, a firebug. Taupo, car theft. And Petone, Ponderosa Day. The scene is set and chummy moves to centre stage."

"Well, that's what the pattern shows. But how'd this fella know Blaney would be at Taupo? Blaney didn't know himself till the last minute. A replacement for George Bagnall when he broke his leg."

"Did he have to know in advance? Or just be there? Blaney was driving the lead police car for the vice-regal party, don't forget. Everywhere the governor-general went, Blaney went. On show almost. And once spotted—well, public knowledge how long the guv was staying at Taupo. Public knowledge he'd be staying at the Lodge. Down the other end of Lake Taupo."

"So anyone could guess he'd be down that end of the Lake. Know exactly where to find him."

"That's right. And anyone could guess Blaney would be under orders to co-operate with Taupo same as Taupo would be under orders to co-operate with the security detail. Anything happen down that end of the Lake, Blaney would be nearest patrol."

"That hurry call from Turangi!"

"It's a possibility. Taupo never did actually pin down who 'phoned in. Let me see——"

Quickly he scanned the report. "Yes. Supposed to come from Bill Pratt, the motel owner. Bill Pratt says no. Bit of trouble in the bar earlier. Not enough for police. They wrote it off as some nervous guest afraid things might get out of hand."

"We could ask for the guest list, for all the good that will do. That's where the reporters, general hangers-on were holed up. Quite a mob. Chances are no one we want to know."

"That's the trouble, of course. Taupo's population must double at Easter. And not all at motels, motor camps, either."

"The sooner we can give them a name——" Steven was interrupted by the telephone, paused to listen to the cheery voice from Lower Hutt.

"Hi, there. Prelim reports from Taupo and Napier. Just off the top of their heads, y'understand, so not complete. Both say they have scads of tourists during the season so just because certain names are marked 'Not known' doesn't mean they've never been there. So, you supply a date and they'll do the hotel motel bit."

Cheerfully said but what a job! Lake Taupo, the great inland sea in the centre of the North Island. Fishermen's paradise. Steven had no idea how many motor camps, motels, lodges dotted the shore of the lake from Taupo at the top to Turangi at the bottom—not even counting the numerous trout streams that would have their full quota of tourist accommodation. It would be easier at Napier, on the east coast. The end of February was hardly holiday season.

Steven supplied the dates, began writing down the meagre

162

information. He handed the listings to Peacock, watched the older man's face cloud as he read.

Napier had marked as known:

BRENDON	Annual leave middle March
BRISTOWE	Father works farm ten miles out. Minor JD. Went to L. Hutt last year. Convicted auto theft. Eighteen months probation.
HEATH	Friendly prop. local restaurant. Visited every other Tuesday till late March
HOUNSELL	Competed and won skin-diving championship held 25-26 February
THOMPSON	Drunk and Disorderly New Year's Eve
WHITE	With family summer vacation end January

Taupo was no better. Their listing showed:

COLLINS	Fishing buff
CUMMING	Cousin prop. Taniwha Lodge. Frequent visitor
HEATH	See earlier reports
THOMPSON	Mother lives Turangi. Frequent visitor long weekends. Heavy drinker
WHITE	Mrs White and Tommy spent Easter here while Dr at seminar Hamilton. Picked family up Tuesday.

Peacock scowled, turned the paper face downwards on the table. "How about Collins' statement? In yet?" He sounded as though he was no longer interested in Napier or Taupo.

"Right here, sir," said Steven. He handed over the report then settled back to his stack of information. Halfway through he headed a blank sheet of paper "Clothes", began to take notes but no one except Cumming and police personnel had been wearing anything blue.

He made a note to investigate where Sigley had been between shortly before ten when Heath left and eleven when he told Bristowe he was going to Lower Hutt.

163

Peacock asked for earlier analyses, began systematically comparing them with source material. They were both immersed in paper work, interrupted only by the entry now and then of a cadet with further reports, when Steven looked up to find Peacock leafing through the photograph album.

Suddenly, Jonas shut the book with a snap, sat tapping the leather cover with thoughtful fingers. He stood up sharply, left the room with the brusque comment, "If I'm needed, I'm with Brian Fairbrother".

Steven slipped back into the paperwork. Most of the information seemed to cover Monday morning, was centred on Tennyson Street, that quiet street ending at the gates of the primary school. All strange cars parked in the immediate area had been accounted for and someone had been diligent enough to check the whereabouts of cars owned by anyone already connected with the case.

After a second reading, Steven placed the study aside. He did not think a car was involved. Granted, there was every likelihood Tommy had been trailed to make sure he did end up at the stopbank but a car would be far more conspicuous than a man on foot, the man Mrs Allen had glimpsed without really noticing.

He ate a snack lunch absently, was reading details of dry cleaners' listings, noting familiar names cropping up, when Jonas entered to remind him of their appointment with the Whites.

"Ready?" he demanded.

"Yes, sir," said Steven, jumping up. "Quite ready."

Peacock paused by the desk to read the first few lines of the interim report. "Everybody's story confirmed, I suppose."

"So far. One or two things though, sir. For instance, ballistics says the gun pulls to the left. A stranger handling it would need to check on its action."

"So what! He had a full clip, didn't he? Only needed one shot for the job. Couple of minutes target practice . . ." He paused. "Ah, yes, see what you mean. Someone might've heard him. Seen him. Won't hurt to inquire along those lines. Let's hope it wasn't out in the hills someplace. Other point?"

164

"A Mrs King in the Jackson Street flats saw a man on the stopbank at ten-twenty-five."

"She's sure of the time?"

"Positive. New baby so she's pretty time conscious right now. Baby's morning feed at half past. She went out to the balcony for some naps she had airing in the sun. Looked along the stopbank and there he was. Walking towards the pavilion. Too far to identify but the description fits."

"He looked like a policeman?"

"Yes. Her exact words, quote 'I thought it was the policeman come back'!"

"Oh, someone been out there earlier?"

"Yes, sir. Call came in at eight-ten." He found the appropriate paper, summarized it.

"Stray horse in distress on the river bank. Ranger wasn't available so one of the uniform men went. The horse was tangled in barbed wire. He freed it, walked it back to the pound."

Peacock eyed him grimly. "All right. You've had your fun. Who was he? The uniform man who went over to the stopbank?"

"Bruce Wilkins."

"Bruce Wilkins, eh?" He looked at his watch, frowning. As if on cue, the door opened, Bruce Wilkins entered, papers in his hand. He hesitated when he saw Peacock, placed the new material in front of Steven.

Peacock said quietly, "Close the door, Wilkins."

Wilkins closed the door, faced Peacock across the narrow table. "I understand you conducted the interview with Collins, Mrs Collins and this next-door neighbour."

"That's correct, sir."

"How did you feel about it? Checking on a colleague?"

Wilkins shrugged. "We're all being checked in this case, sir. Me included. My statement's one of those." He indicated the new additions.

"Ah, yes. Something about a horse. Why pick you?"

"Used to animals, sir. Brought up on a farm."

"Which means you ride and so forth."

"Yes, sir."

165

"It's a wonder you didn't get the job of being a bandit."

"I was considered, sir, but——" His hand touched his blond near-white hair. "They decided a dark-haired man."

"So Blaney got the job. Now, this Mrs King saw you earlier so when she saw this other man she said, quote, 'I thought it was the policeman come back,' unquote. But you were?"

"At Wedell's, sir. Factory on TePuni Street. Call came in at nine-forty-eight. One of the girls went—well, she attacked the forewoman. No damage beyond a few scratches. Just an upset. The secretary rang, for advice mainly. Didn't want to lay charges. Tolliver and I went down, smoothed things over, waited with the girl till her pay was made up, took her home."

"I see," Peacock seemed a trifle disappointed. "Well, at least we've had two sightings of our friend so we have a fair idea of what he looks like. How tall are you, Wilkins?"

"Six foot one, sir."

"And you were wearing summer uniform and no cap?"

"That's correct, sir. Went on Moorhead's bike. A nice day and it wasn't, well, official."

"Right. So we're looking for a tall man, dressed in dark trousers, light blue shirt or jacket, probably fair or grey hair. Bald even. Get that description out to the men on house to house. Ask about this man. Especially around the Tennyson Street area. And get out a public request. Ask for anyone who remembers seeing Tommy talking to a man of that description. Not so much the clothes but the rest of it. Particularly on Ponderosa Day."

"Yes, sir. I'll see to that right away."

"By the way, Wilkins. Did you find the horse's owner?"

"Yes, sir. A Miss Pauline Summers. Seaview Pony Club. Leases that paddock behind the golf course for grazing. And maybe you noticed, the fences need repairing."

When the door closed, Peacock turned to Steven. "Well, that's not going to eliminate anyone much, is it?"

"Sigley maybe. Cumming's around five eight. Might scrape through and his clothes were right. The only one so far."

"Except for police personnel, of course. Well, we'd better get moving. Nearly one o'clock."

166

They found the Whites in the small secluded area at the back of the house. Mrs White was reclining in a chaise longue, face shaded, body slack in the full heat of the sun, while the professor was attacking the enclosing hedge with inexperienced clippers.

He stopped immediately he saw them, placed the clippers carefully on top of a small stepladder. "Not my job really, but while old Jonsey was away, thought I'd give it a try."

Steven was shocked by Mrs White's appearance. She lay there, eyes closed, lines of grief and tiredness etched deep on her face, thin hands quiet against the edge of the chair.

Peacock murmured greetings and the dark eyelids fluttered. She sat up, smoothed her skirts in a self-conscious action.

"D'you want to talk here or inside?" asked Peacock.

Mrs White looked at her husband, waiting his decision. White glanced at the hedge, thick and compact, giving an impression of privacy that was not complete. "Perhaps we'd better go inside."

Mrs White stood up, led the way into the coolness of that vast kitchen. Steven realized with a start that all the time they had been there she had not spoken a word.

Now she sat in a cane chair, a boldly-striped cushion at her back, the men grouped around her like a class in Sunday School. Steven watched the professor who was studying his wife so intently that he jumped when Peacock spoke.

"Sorry to bother you. But I'm afraid there's certain information that you, and you alone, can give us, Mrs White. This morning I went to consult Dr Fraser, not realizing he was Tommy's doctor."

Mrs White brought her eyes from far distances. She frowned but made no comment, showed no surprise, no interest.

"I consulted him about Tommy in an oblique way," he ploughed on. "No names. Not much detail. But he recognized the case. A fine example, he said, of how care and attention can extend the life of the patient."

Mrs White gave a tremulous smile, shook her head, face puckered, eyes closing in pain.

White intervened. "Inspector, d'you think this is wise?"

Peacock waved him aside impatiently. "Mrs White!" he said

sharply—and the sad eyes opened, focused vaguely on his face. "Dr Fraser warned you to notify him immediately if Tommy showed any schizophrenic tendencies yet you failed to do so. Why?"

Mrs White did not answer. Her eyes dropped to her lap where her fingers played with a handkerchief, folding, unfolding, folding, unfolding.

"Mrs White! Answer me!" And Steven was startled by the harshness of his voice. "You were the one who told Tommy he was on no account to tell anyone who the people he called 'they' were. You warned him he wasn't to mention hearing voices to anyone—didn't you? Didn't you?"

The tired eyes lifted defiantly, the back straightened. "Yes, I was the one, Inspector. I told him it was something he wasn't to mention to anyone—to anyone. Y'see, it meant there was nothing—that Tommy—— Don't you see—they would have taken Tommy away—away——"

CHAPTER XIX

"N O. N O. S T O P T H A T!" shouted White, stepping in front of his wife. His voice dropped to a more conciliatory tone. "She can't take much more. Please let her be."

Peacock's face was granite. "I'm sorry, but Mrs White must talk to us. We realize she was trying to protect Tommy in the beginning. Now she's simply protecting Tommy's murderer."

"Murderer!" White jerked as though slapped. "But Bob said——"

"Yes, Dr Whittaker said drowned. That's the way it looked. But since then we've established that Tommy was unconscious when he was placed in the water."

White moved away from his wife, looked down at her.

"Murdered!" she whispered.

"I'm afraid so. Look, Mrs White. We believe someone's been talking to Tommy. For quite a while. He told Tommy to go to Gregg's. He told Tommy to climb the mountain and go to the stopbank. And Tommy obeyed because he was used to him. Make sense to you, Mrs White?"

"It makes sense. It had to be that way. I couldn't understand why Tommy—but someone he was used to——"

"So you see that's why we need to talk to you. Particularly about the whispers."

"You—you knew?"

"Yes. But we didn't understand the significance then. Now we do. When did Tommy first mention the whispers, Mrs White?"

"The day before his birthday. 17 October."

A month ago. Something clicked in Steven's brain. A month

ago someone found the Luger in Hounsell's room.

"Did you ever hear this voice, Mrs White?"

"Well, I listened one night, to please Tommy. But—it was nothing really. A sighing—a long drawn out whispering as though someone was calling Tommy, Tommy . . ." She lowered her voice to a whisper, drawling the words to a sigh. "I went to the window and looked out. But there was nothing. No one in sight. I—I rationalized it. Said it was only the wind."

"You said one night. And you looked out of a window."

"Yes, Tommy's window. Just after seven. He isn't—wasn't very strong. That's why he went to bed early. I'd read him a story, tuck him in. Sometimes he'd still be awake when I looked in later but at least he was resting."

"Always at night? The whispers?"

She hesitated. "I—I don't know. There was one time in the afternoon. Y'see, I told Tommy he was not to say anything to anyone but he could talk to me. And he did. It was just now and then at first. And he talked about toys, books, guns."

"The guns he kept in his room? Handguns? Wheellocks?"

"Yes. Mostly about guns. Later, it was, well, every day he was telling me something. Stories almost."

"You said the whispers came mostly at night, so Tommy told you either before he went to sleep or first thing in the morning —as though he had dreamed about it. But once it was in the afternoon. D'you remember the day?"

She shook her head. "All I remember it was drizzling so Tommy played in his room. He came into the studio where I was working, started talking about the whisperer. Nothing special. Guns. Sheriffs. Cowboys."

"And this last week he's been talking bandits and bank robbers. Is that so?"

"Yes. But we told him about Ponderosa Day. I knew these ministry officials were coming so I'd have to be there. But I thought Tommy would enjoy the excitement up town. As long as he didn't believe it was real."

"So when he started talking bandits, you thought it was because of what you told him. Even when he told you one of the bandits was going to make a break for the hideaway."

"But Mr Cumming must've told him that."

"He knew. But did he tell Tommy? That's something we have to establish. When did Tommy mention it to you?"

"Monday. Tuesday. Monday, Tommy went fishing with Mr Cumming. Tuesday we went to the doctor. That's it. Tuesday morning. Just before we went. I—I spoke to him about the whispers and he told me then. It must've been Mr Cumming."

"Cumming didn't know himself till Tuesday afternoon. You're quite sure it was Tuesday morning?"

"I'm sure." She flushed. averted her eyes. "Y'see, I didn't want Tommy saying anything to the doctor. That's why—that's why I mentioned it. To warn him again."

"Did he ever say where the hideaway was?"

"No. But he was talking about some big secret he knew. A secret he wasn't to tell anyone. Perhaps that was the secret."

Peacock nodded. "Possible. Well, I think the next step would be a visit to Tommy's room. May we?"

White climbed slowly to his feet, led the way up the stairs, Peacock and Steven following. The room seemed unchanged from the last time Steven had seen it, bed under the window, bedside table almost covered by handguns.

Peacock walked across the room, stared at the wall of Hudson House. The blinds were down on the back-to-back windows opposite but the rooms below were unshaded.

He knelt on the bed to lean out of the window, examined the ivy ladder closely, shook his head, straightened. He looked at the guns, hefting each one in turn to judge the weight.

"Well, that's that," said Peacock. "I think we've seen all we want, Dr White. Except—I'd like to look at Tommy's mountain from ground level. Can we borrow that step-ladder?"

"Of course. Help yourself."

They followed White down to the porch where Jenny White was bending over the pumice containers, studying the silken petals of a pale yellow flower on one of the miniature plants.

"Look, Alex," she said in a lilting voice. "There's a flower on it. And I never even noticed."

She held her hand out to White, smiled up to his face. Steven and Peacock withdrew discreetly, found the step-ladder and Jonas mounted it, looked closely at the ivy, tested a few metal inserts.

Bruce Wilkins had news for them on their return. "House to house turned up a witness, sir. Saw Blueshirt. A Mr Roberts. On the 'phone now, sir."

Peacock hurried into the office, picked up one telephone, nodded to Steven to take the other. "Mr Roberts? Inspector Peacock. I understand you've seen a man in blue."

"Yes. That's right, Inspector. Working on that new rockery of mine when this guy goes loping past. Not running, y'know. But walking fast. Stripped down I was, because it was so hot. And here's this guy—hands in pockets, collar turned up. Like it was cold. Had a second look because I just couldn't believe it. Didn't see him face on, y'understand, but I'd know him again see him soon enough. Sure I'd know him."

"Did he notice you?"

"Don't think so. Having a breather, y'know. Hunkered down against the fence. On the south side. Close palings. Five foot high. Looked up, sort of, when I heard the footsteps. Watched till he got in front of Struthers there. Couldn't see where he went. Struthers' garage out front. Blocks the view. Sure. Sure I'd know him. Like I said. See him soon enough."

Peacock pulled the sketch map towards him, spoke to Wilkins. "Right. Roberts saw Blueshirt here. Struthers, I presume, is the corner house. That means, one, he continued on along this street to Ava Station or, two, he turned into this street here. Any other reports in?"

"Some, but not helpful. The houses towards Ava, nothing. This street—mostly factories, storerooms. No windows overlooking."

"Well, keep plugging. Looks as though he's moving away from the shopping centre. Could've gone into one of the houses around there. Could've discarded the blue jacket. Roberts said jacket, not a shirt?"

"Definitely a jacket, sir."

"Might be a good idea to search around. He'd know the blue
172

would be noticed. Discard that—a different description."

"Could be he wore one of those blue nylon overjackets they wear in shops. Hairdressers. Fold up to this size. Put it in his pocket easy enough."

Peacock thought about that. "Possible. Talk to Mrs King, Mrs Allen again. Make sure about the colour. And Roberts, ask him about that jacket. Cloth. Open or done up. Then around three-thirty pick him up, stake out Hudson House. See if he recognizes anyone."

Bruce Wilkins had hardly left on his errands before he was back again. "Fellow to see you, sir. About the Blaney case."

Peacock looked up wearily. "Can't you handle it, Wilkins?"

"Name of Craddock, sir. John Craddock."

Peacock looked at Steven. Steven looked at Peacock, "Craddock? Blaney's mate from Napier? Send him in."

Craddock entered diffidently. Young, thin-faced, dark-eyed, hair already receding at the temples. He glanced swiftly around the small room before taking the proffered chair.

"Good of you to come in," said Peacock. "We did ask Napier to check certain points but we didn't expect to see you."

"Up for my brother's wedding, sir. A week's leave." He hesitated. "I'm stationed at Queenstown, now, sir, so I'm afraid I don't know what you wanted to check."

Peacock rubbed his chin thoughtfully. "So you've come in off your own bat? Got something to tell us?"

"I think so, sir. It's just—just a hunch though."

"Could be what we're waiting for. Relax, Craddock. Take your time and talk easy."

Craddock chewed his lip. "Well, sir, as I said, I'm on leave. And you know how it is. I've been wandering around looking up old cobbers and so on. Last night, well, last night there was a mob of us at the Central—yarning, y'know. And there was a lull in the conversation. Reg had gone up to the bar for a couple more jars and we were kind of waiting. I started looking around, see if I could spot anyone else I knew. Y'know, old home week. And I saw this fellow down at the end of the bar. Had his back to me but seemed familiar."

"I was craning for a better look but just then Reg came back

173

with the jars and, well, I guess I forgot about him. This fellow, I mean."

"Early in the evening? Seven—seven-thirty?"

Craddock blinked. "Yes, sir. Just after seven. Ten, maybe quarter past. No later. I did have a looksee later on. But he'd gone." His eyes dropped to his hands rubbing gently together. "Then—then, this morning, round about three, I think, I woke up with a start. And it was all there. On a plate. Who this fellow was. Joe's death. The lot. I—I suppose you think that's crazy."

"No. Happens. Go to bed with a problem. Wake up in the middle of the night with the answer. But you hit the jackpot."

"Think so. Everything fits. I've been mulling it over all morning. Trying to find the holes. Only thing, I can't figure why."

"We'll tell you why," said Peacock. "You tell us how."

Craddock frowned, shrugged. "Well, sir, this is what I think. I think someone tried to kill Joe before. At Napier. A run-in with the firebug. At least, that's what we thought at the time but now—now I know Joe was set up."

"You do?" Peacock sighed. "We've had a look at that but, well, fellow wasn't there at the right time."

"He was there all right," said Craddock grimly. "Y'see, there's this restaurant. Romanoff's. Supposed to be Russian, so everyone working there sports a Russian handle."

He laughed softly. "A gimmick, y'know, to give the place atmosphere. The owner wears the name Oleg Romanoff but his real name's Craddock. Lewis Craddock. My uncle. We used to eat there. In the kitchen so people wouldn't spot police all over."

"Joe Blaney?"

"Yes, Joe Blaney and other guys flatting like us. Anyway, we got to know the staff pretty well and this guy, well, he used to come in and work with the underchef."

"Every other Tuesday?"

"More or less. Day off at his own show, he said. Anyway, often as not, he'd drift over. Have a chat. Quite talkative and interested in police doings. Asked him once if he'd ever been police but he laughed, said police used his restaurant, talked shop and he listened. Well, that week in February—everything

174

happened. Benning, the underchef, got mugged Monday night. Landed up in hospital. So when this guy turns up Tuesday and finds Benning off for a few days, he offered to pitch in."

"Did he though! Tell us about this mugging, Craddock. First we've heard about it."

"Well, it went like this, sir. Benning woke up in the middle of the night, saw this shadow coming at him. Before he could yell or anything fellow jumped him. Roughed him up good and proper. Benning reckons he came to about an hour later. Wasn't able to move, get help, till daybreak."

"You think there's a connection?"

"Well, we never did clear that up, sir. And now, well, I guess we could establish he knew where Benning lived—the bach is pretty isolated. And he'd know Benning was a bit of a soak. Guess he'd go to bed half stoned. Be too dopey to resist. Of course we wouldn't be able to prove any of this now, but——"

"It all fits in. Anything else?"

"Yes, sir. Maybe nothing in it but Wednesday night we were talking about scares we'd had. I told them about one night at Torson's. Eerie place, sir. Quiet as death. Right on the edge of town. Away from everyone. Well, this night I thought I heard something. Stood there listening. Next thing this damn big cat jumped down behind me. Nearly threw me for six. Got a big laugh. Then I said—I said, 'Could've been someone who meant business'. Could've beaten me up and left me for dead and no one would've found me till morning." His eyes were troubled. "D'you think that's what gave him the idea, sir?"

"Hardly. Gave him a jolt perhaps but he must've had it all planned before the Benning business. When did you go on nights?"

"Started 6th February."

"Yes, and another wood-yard fire on the 12th. This time with traces. So two-hour checks ordered. An extra job. Grizzled about it, did you?"

"Some, I guess. Didn't take so long to scoot around. But on top of everything else—a nuisance. Joe and I alternated. If I did the nine o'clock, he'd do the eleven, me one and so on. Next night we'd swap over."

"So a watcher could easily establish your pattern."

"Afraid so. You think he was watching us?"

"Possible. Now, Blaney did the three o'clock Tuesday, Thursday, Saturday that week. Tuesday, still monitoring maybe. Thursday, well, Wednesday you did your piece. Saturday probably his first choice anyway. Water carnival on the foreshore, wasn't there? Big influx of visitors. Good cover."

"Last chance anyway. Benning was back on Monday."

"Right. So he missed out at Napier. Had to follow Blaney to Petone. He'd know Blaney was posted to Petone?"

"Surely. Postings aren't secret. Besides, I'd hoped for Petone or Lower Hutt. Ribbed Joe for pinching my spot."

"So it had to be Petone. Meantime, Taupo. I think that one was off the cuff. All arrangements made then Blaney turned up. That misfired anyway. So down to Petone. And right next door— Tommy White."

Peacock fell silent, frowning in concentration. Steven began to think of Tommy White, how his life had changed that last month.

The whispers started, telling him stories of adventure. At first, Tommy was puzzled. He even told his mother, and his mother said it was the wind. But the whispers were real to Tommy. Real. They spoke of cowboys, rustlers, bandits, guns— always guns.

Steven could imagine the boy crouched at his windowsill listening. He would stare at the blank wall of Hudson House not realizing that, behind the drawn blind, a man was talking to him. For 30 days Tommy listened to that voice, his constant companion.

Last week the voice told him about bank robbers, about a bandit who was going to hide at Gregg's, in the hideaway above the garage. If Tommy went there at the right time, he could capture the bandit. He would be a hero. But it was a secret. No one must know about the hideaway. Only Tommy. And he would be told when to go there.

Tommy was told on Ponderosa Day. He set off, taking the long way round while his advisor took the shorter route through the recreation grounds, lifted the key from the cistern, entered

176

Gregg's kitchen, in position before Tommy arrived. Tommy would not think it strange when the whispers started. He had long since accepted the voice as part of his life—a friend, a storyteller, a bringer of adventure.

The voice told him to wait, wait, till the bandit came. So Tommy waited, listening to the voice. He played with the sand piled by the wind. He found the key on the patio, buried it under the hydrangea, scattered marigolds he had plucked through the wire as he passed his home.

The bandit came—and was shot. He fell from the stairs and lay still. Still. Nothing else happened. The whispers stopped—and the bandit lay still and quiet. Quiet.

In the distance Tommy could hear the noises of Ponderosa Day. It meant something. Excitement. Crowds. He left the bandit, the silence, started to run along the drive of chipped brick—and found the Luger. That was right, too. They had promised him a gun and here it was. He picked it up, aimed it, decided to keep it.

Then the questioning started. Everyone was asking questions. His mother. His father. Big men with strange faces. And the voice no longer talked to him. He was alone. Alone with all the questioning. Alone with all this misery inside him—and his mother saying, play with the boats. He allowed her to lead him to the bath half filled with water, stubbornly refusing to talk. As soon as she left, he picked up his yacht, the cabin cruiser, crept into his room where he crouched by the window wishing, wishing he could go outside into the lovely sunshine and play.

Then he heard the voice again, whispering about the fun of sailing boats at the stopbank. Come to the stopbank. We can be together. We can sail your boats. Don't tell Mummy. She's cross. Let it be a surprise. Climb down the mountain. That's easy. Climb down and we'll meet at the stopbank. And sail the boats. Climb down, climb down, climb down——

And Tommy had climbed down his mountain, had gone to the stopbank to meet the only "friend" he had left in the world.

Peacock sighed heavily. "Yes, that must be what happened. He decided to make use of Tommy White. Probably had some-

177

thing planned for the end of November and Ponderosa Day fell into his lap."

"Stupid though. Trying to beat the law of averages."

"I guess he thought he had us licked. Got away with it twice and the third time—we can't prove that either. Probably thought he was home and dry then Hounsell put his spoke in."

"Hounsell?"

"Yes. Told us about the gun. I bet he thought Hounsell would keep quiet. Illegal gun and all that. But he didn't—and next thing we are investigating Hudson House. Suddenly he didn't feel so secure. Tommy was a potential danger."

Steven noted Peacock's scowl, said carefully. "Won't be easy proving he's Blueshirt, sir. Even with an ident. from Roberts. Those two fellows in town said he was wearing grey. Sigley, too. Goes in for grey. Had another jacket at the cleaners that day. Grey jacket, brown trousers, the docket said."

"We'll find a way," growled Peacock. "And we need to tidy up Mrs King. She said she saw Blueshirt on the stopbank at twenty-five past yet he caught the half-past bus."

"May I interrupt, sir," Craddock interposed diffidently. "There are two bus services in Petone. The railway bus from outlying areas to the station and the Eastbourne bus to Wellington through Petone. Has to go around the bays first. Takes about twenty minutes. The half-past bus would be the half-past from Eastbourne. Goes through Petone about ten to eleven."

"Oh? That's better. Gives him time to make a feint towards Ava, double back to Jackson Street."

He looked up as Bruce Wilkins entered. "About the gun, sir. One of our fellows lives next door to the secretary of the local pistol club. Says the lock of the clubrooms was tampered with. Only happened to mention it because Peterson's police."

"When did she notice it?"

"Friday night, sir. But everything in order when she opened up. Peterson's taking her back to the clubrooms. Having a closer look."

"A bit late, isn't it?"

"Might not be, sir. Peterson says the targets set up in front of a concrete wall. Spent bullets accumulate in between. Every so often they hold a working bee to reclaim the lead. Next one scheduled for Saturday week."

"Well, they'd better do it now. Send a couple of men down to give them a hand. They know what to look for. Where are the clubrooms anyhow?"

"On the riverbank, sir. Close by the place where we found the bits and pieces out of Hounsell's room."

"Is that so? You think he did the pistol practice and discarded the loot at the same time. Possible—but when?"

"When, sir?"

"Yes. Not in the daytime. Be noticed. Nights he works. Company provides transport to and fro. Mmmm. Get hold of Stacey's. See if Heath had any time off Thursday night."

"Heath!" Wilkins let go a low whistle. "You mean, he took the gun and the loot to work Thursday night?"

"Why not? Be safe enough in his locker. But how did he carry it. Not in his pockets. Any ideas, Wilkins?"

"Yes, sir. Carries a duffelbag. Had it with him last night when we brought them in. Asked me if he could leave it at the desk while in with you. Said, sure, nothing of value, is it? And he said, 'No, just work clothes'."

"Work clothes?"

"Yes. I quizzed Thompson on that one. Seems he carts work clothes to and from, to wear under overalls. Morning has a shower, changes back into his fancy duds." He hesitated. "You must've noticed his clothes, sir. Doesn't buy anything off the hook. Everything tailored. Follows trends like nobody's business."

"Ah, yes, a friend of yours, isn't he?"

"Not exactly. Met him once or twice at Hudson House. That's all. But the fellows talk a bit. Got him taped as a spender. Y'know, best of everything for himself and money no object."

"We'll have to keep that in mind," said Peacock drily. "Now, Wilkins, if you'll get in touch with Stacey's——"

"On my way, sir." As soon as the door closed behind Wilkins, Peacock turned to Craddock.

"I suppose you're still interested in the cockeyed reason behind all this, eh? Well, like you we had already noticed the tie-in.

179

Napier, Taupo, Petone. And we also had this——" He placed the album in front of Craddock opened to show the newspaper photograph.

"I couldn't remember the circumstances so I had a long talk with Brian Fairbrother. He's senior sergeant in charge here and a close friend of the Blaneys." He paused, shut the book, put it aside. "D'you remember that juvenile gang in Auckland? Called themselves the Red Rebels?"

"The Red Rebels? Killed an old woman and two youngsters, didn't they? The Armed Offenders Squad had to go into the Waitakeri Ranges after them."

"That's right. The Rebels held out for ten hours. Two officers were injured. One Rebel killed. His name—Gregory Pearce Miller. Alias Scuddy Heath. Or more precisely, né Gregory Pearce Heath."

"You mean—— His son!"

"Yes. His son. Auckland interviewed Mrs Miller, of course. Seems she married Miller a couple of years after the divorce. Scuddy would be about five. And the only contact his natural father ever had with the boy after that was a present every birthday. Usually something extravagantly expensive. Upset the boy no end. Got the idea his father was rich whereas Miller was just making a go of it."

He was interrupted by the door opening. Moorhead looked in, said firmly, "Chief Inspector Blaney to see you, sir."

"Of course. Send him in." He turned to Craddock. "Chief Inspector Blaney was in charge of the squad who captured the Red Rebels, did you know? And that's what this is all about. Thanks for coming in, Craddock. Gave us that much head start. And Sergeant, get on to Taupo. See what they have to say."

Steven and Craddock left, passing Inspector Blaney in the doorway.

CHAPTER XX

TAUPO. AND SERGEANT Henare Watene.

"Yeh. Met him first time when he came with the guv. Spoke to him coupla times. Y'know, locals looking out for the specials. But mostly they were down at the other end of the lake. And only a few days at that."

"This accident Blaney had. We've decided it was an attempted murder."

"Come off it, Sarge. Just some hairy galoot fancied someone else's car. That's all!"

"I repeat, Sergeant. We think it was a murder attempt. We have a name. We have a motive. Now, gear your thinking along those lines and see what you come up with."

"You're serious!" Pause. "Come to think of it. First time I've ever seen a car slung across the road like that. Blaney couldn't have missed it. Wonder he wasn't killed. Oh! Oh! That's it, of course. He should've been killed."

"The driver of the stolen car got clean away?"

"Didn't hang around, that's for sure. Didn't leave any traces either. No dabs. Nothing."

"And if Blaney had steered right, he'd have gone over the edge of the cliff. Right? So how d'you feel about attempted murder?"

"Yeh. Yeh. Could be a set up at that. Besides, we never did find out who sent in that hurry call."

"Our friend, perhaps?"

"Dicey. My guess, he was tailing Blaney waiting till the traffic was thin enough to pull his stunt. Blaney said something about a black car, way back. A Mercedes, he thought."

"That wasn't mentioned in the report."

"Well, no. Blaney didn't think too much of it. Said it followed

181

him up from Turangi then turned off. Into one of those motor camps, he thought. Next thing, this other car—whoosh!"

"This stolen car. Did it come from that area?"

"Right on. Couple of doors away from the motor camp. That's why we gave all the bods there the once over."

"The family were away, the report said. Leave their car behind?"

"No. No. Took the station wagon. Left the roadster. Garage, one of those basement types. Y'know. Two-car garage and rumpus room with the entrance hall between. A window in the rumpus room jemmied."

"But only the car was taken?"

"Only the car." Pause. "Yeh, I get what you mean. Why not do over the whole house while on the job?"

"Did the family leave keys with anyone?"

"Yes. A friend in town. Fellow by the name of Maurice Thawley. Runs a restaurant along the road here."

"Oh? Where did he keep the key?"

"In the till. Leastways, that's where it was when we asked for it."

"Thank you, Sergeant. That all ties in. Maurice Thawley's partner is Charles Lederer Heath. And we believe Heath engineered this accident."

"Not on your nellie. He was busy having an accident himself that night. Other side of Taupo. Couldn't have been at Hatepe and on Mapara Road at the same time."

"You're sure it was the same night?"

"Sure I'm sure. Saw the insurance claim, didn't I?"

"Tell me about it. You don't make a habit of checking insurance claims, do you?"

"No, but, well, there was this hit-and-run. Easter Sunday. Little girl badly hurt. So we checked garages, y'know. Turned up Heath's car. Not much damage. Head light. Bumper bar. But we needed to know. Told us it happened Monday night. Seems he delivered this gun he'd fixed for a friend on Mapara Road. Family gone to bed by the time he got there so he left the gun on the porch. On the way back, he clipped this telegraph pole."

182

"You confirmed everything he claimed, no doubt?"

"We did. Thawley said the car was okay Monday so that let him out of the hit-and-run. And this guy he fixed the gun for—Watson—confirmed he found the gun on his porch as stated. Even had a look at the post that stepped in front of him."

"Any witnesses?"

"You kidding! At that time of night! Nothing so lonely as a country road at night."

"Okay! I'll accept the fact that he damaged his car. That it happened on the other side of Taupo. But as far as the actual time—— He could've done it any time right up to five or six in the morning."

"Granted. But we'd never be able to prove it."

"We won't be trying to prove it. Just want to satisfy ourselves in our own minds. Now, you said he fixed this chap's gun. Does a bit of tinkering, does he?"

"Hardly tinkering. Expert gunsmith. Crack shot. The lot!"

"And he drives a black Mercedes. Right?"

"Yes, but—— I see, the black Mercedes that followed Blaney that night."

"It's a wonder he didn't sell the car. Save him traipsing all the way down to Petone."

"He did sell the car. Part of the down payment for this deal they had going. That the lot?"

"Not quite. In February he was absent from the restaurant for a few days. Remember?"

"February—mmm—that's right. Suspected hepatitis. Or something. Maurie was fit to be tied. Almost tearing his hair out. Pleased as hell when it turned out the doc. was a bit over cautious. Let me see, the last week in February it would be. Stayed with some relation in Taradale. Any good to you?"

"Right on, as you say. Well, have another look at that accident, Sergeant. Let us have your conclusions."

Steven knocked on the door, entered to catch the end of the conversation. Peacock was perched on the end of the table, bending solicitously towards Blaney who looked grey and shrunken.

183

"He could've asked," said Blaney wearily. "He had plenty contacts. And he was entitled to know."

"But he didn't ask. Wasn't the type. Mrs Miller told us that. Broods, she said. Gets a bee in his bonnet and nothing can shift it. Doesn't want to know the truth. Not if it means he's wrong. So he keeps it to himself. Nurses it along till it's the mainspring of his life. An obsession to pay back in kind."

"Yes, I get that bit. An eye for an eye. His son so my son. But will he stop there? I'm not the only man on the squad with a son. If we can't make this one stick——"

Blaney stopped, aware at last of Steven's presence. "Sorry, Sergeant. Holding things up, am I?"

"Not at all, sir. But maybe you'll be interested in this further information from Taupo."

Briefly he detailed the significant evidence. He had hardly finished when Bruce Wilkins entered triumphantly. "Stacey's say Heath knocked off at five-thirty Friday morning. Never worked short time before."

Peacock nodded. "Seems we need another talk with Mr Heath."

Inspector Blaney touched his arm. "May I come? I won't be in the way. I promise."

Peacock hesitated, then agreed. It was the least he could do.

The stake-out car was still in place near Hudson House when they arrived. Moorhead, who was sitting it out with Roberts, made a discreet signal.

Alan Bristowe emerged from the wide gates, began to walk towards the township. He saw the police car, hesitated as Peacock climbed out followed closely by Steven and Blaney.

"Hello, Alan," said Peacock genially. "Can you spare a minute? One or two questions. About Ponderosa Day. Now, d'you remember seeing Tommy White about the time of the robbery?"

"Yes, sir. Passed him on the way down town. Y'see, I used the 'phone in Siggy's office. To call my ma. At the front, y'know, so I came out this way. Passed Tommy just about here."

"Talk to him at all?"

"Yes. I said, 'You're going the wrong way, tiger. All the fun's up town.' And he just gave me that funny smile of his. Said something about a bandit."

"But you didn't know what he meant?"

"No. Now, well, I guess that's when he went to Gregg's."

"In which case, why didn't he go through the rec?"

"Oh, no, Tommy wouldn't do that. He always stuck to foot-paths."

"I see. Now, you saw Charlie Heath too. When exactly?"

"When he came up to us after. Y'know, like I said. He helped us with the boxes."

"You also said he was watching the show from the crowd in front of you. Didn't you see him then?"

"Nooooo."

"Then how did you know he was in the crowd?"

"Well, he told me, like. I mean, well, he just told me. That's all."

"He told you." Peacock nodded. "Well, we won't keep you any longer, Alan." A car door opened and shut. They turned to see Moorhead walking towards them, waited till the constable joined them. "No luck?" asked Peacock.

"Not so far, sir. Roberts is getting a bit restive. Wants to know if he can turn it in. Go home."

Peacock grimaced. "Yeh, maybe we did start a bit too early, but I didn't want to take any chances. Ask him to give us another hour."

He was interrupted by a loud cry. "There he is, Inspector! That's him! The one on the steps!"

For an eternal fraction of time they stood frozen, Roberts pointing towards Hudson House, the four police officers on the footpath, and Charlie Heath in the act of descending the shallow steps.

Heath moved first. At the instant of recovery he was out of sight again, lost in the shadows of Hudson House.

"Get him!" yelled Peacock. The four men pounded along the pavement, through the wide gate, up the steps into the dim hall, rushed through to the back of the premises, the kitchen, where they found a dazed Sigley picking himself up from the floor.

"Seen Heath?" rasped Peacock.

"Yeh. Barged right into me. Went out the back way, I think. What the hell's going on?"

Peacock ignored Sigley, turned to Steven and Moorhead. "Go on. After him. We'll bring the car around."

Steven and Moorhead raced out the back door, through the dusty yard to the gate in the galvanized iron fence. It was jammed for some reason but some hefty pushes soon remedied that. They sped along the lane at the side of the engineering section, paused at the entrance to the recreational grounds.

"There he is!" cried Moorhead, pointing to the figure of Heath on the far side of the playing fields.

Steven started running again, Moorhead plodding doggedly at his shoulder. Straight across the grassed area, the bitumen path, into the shadow of the grandstand, through the gates on to Britannia Street, paused.

There was no sign of Heath. No sign of anybody. The street was lined with parked cars but the only people in sight were 200 yards away, hurrying along Jackson Street, totally uninterested in what was happening in Britannia Street.

A man in post-office uniform sauntered out of the Azalea Court Flats. He was looking at a clip board in his hand but when he reached the edge of the footpath, he looked up, sent a puzzled glance left and right, lifted a hand to scratch his head.

Steven moved over quickly. "Something wrong?" he asked.

"Yes. My van! Had it parked right here. Now it's gone."

"Your own van? Or a post-office van?"

"Post-office, of course." The man looked from Steven to Moorhead. "Say, who are you? Police?"

"Yes," said Steven. "And it seems the fellow we were chasing got away with your van."

The man explained how he had left the van with engine running while he delivered a parcel. Once too often. He was giving Steven the number and description when Peacock and Blaney arrived, tumbled out of the car, ran over to them.

"What's up?" asked Peacock crisply. "You lost him?"

Steven told him the story briefly.

"So you have lost him!" growled Peacock.

"Temporarily," said Steven. "Did you see a red van?"

186

"Didn't pass anything at all," said Peacock grimly.

"So he didn't go north. And south he'd strike Jackson Street. My guess is west. And he'd keep to the back streets."

Peacock looked at him speculatively. "Well, it's worth a try."

Steven drove while Moorhead sent out an alert for the van. Twice they stopped to ask pedestrians if they had seen the van, begrudging every wasted minute but grateful when both replies proved they were going in the right direction.

They arrived at Hutt Road. Steven brought the car to a stop, looked north, looked south. There was no sign of the post-office van in the rushing traffic. Which way? Which way?

South was Wellington, but Heath would be vulnerable all the time he was driving along the Hutt Road where it followed the curve of the harbour, sea on one side, bush-clad hills on the other.

North was Lower Hutt with side streets for easy evasion all the way. As if to confirm his choice of Lower Hutt, the radio suddenly stuttered into life. A police car had sighted the van on Railway Avenue, was following as instructed.

Steven swung the car on to the Hutt Road, weaving a quick route through the traffic.

"Van turned on to Normandale bypass," said the radio.

The bypass soared over roads, railway lines, to connect Lower Hutt with its hilly suburb, Normandale. After a few minutes they reached a point where they could see the whole length of the long overbridge. At the far end was a flash of red that could have been the van.

"Van turning on to Normandale Road," said the radio.

Steven sent the police car on to the bypass, lifting his eyes briefly to the zig-zag road climbing the hill but he could not pick out anything that might be the van.

"Van involved in accident," said the radio laconically.

"Where? What happened?" rasped Peacock, leaning forward.

Moorhead queried the accident report but the relay could not elaborate. The driver of the pursuing car had called in—smashup —then apparently left the car to assist. The relay added as an afterthought that there were council workmen clearing a slip on the Normandale Road in the general vicinity of the accident.

The police car surged up the hill road, one bend then the next, and the next. They saw the "Road Works" warning sign before they swung round the final bend.

Steven braked sharply, his quick eyes taking in the scene ahead—warning notices and drums, drums to reduce the road to a single lane, two of the drums lying on their sides. A group of men clustered around the red van smashed into an unrecognizable mass against the flank of a huge yellow bulldozer.

The police driver left the group, hurried over as they climbed out of their vehicle. The council men drifted away to reform at the edge of the road.

"What happened?" demanded Peacock.

"They tried to stop him, sir. Flagged him down. But he wouldn't be stopped. Hit that first drum there. Knocked that second one over. Sort of bounced off that then slambang into the side of the dozer. I've sent for an ambulance, sir. And notified the fire brigade. He'll have to be cut out."

"Still alive?"

"Yes, sir. Lucky. Passenger side took most of the impact. But he's caught there. Can't move him. Ribs busted for sure. Leg, too. Maybe both legs. Can't tell. Van's sort of pressing in on top of him."

Steven moved over to the wrecked van, peered through the twisted metal and smashed glass at the imprisoned man. Someone had wiped his face, reducing the blood from numerous cuts to a slow ooze, had loosened his tie, unzipped his windbreaker.

As if sensing his presence, Heath opened his eyes. "Hi, Sarge," he said weakly. "Come to gloat?"

"Not at all," said Steven. "Just to let you know the ambulance is on the way. We'll have you out in no time."

Heath's lips writhed. "Fire," he said hoarsely.

"Relax. There's no petrol spill. You'd smell it."

Heath nodded, closed his eyes. Steven watched silently, decided there was nothing he could do, turned to leave, and banged into Inspector Blaney who was standing behind him.

"Sorry, Inspector. Didn't see you. Take over, eh?"

He joined Peacock who was talking to the council foreman, waited, listening to the sound of the approaching ambulance.

Peacock ended his conversation, looked at him inquiringly.

"As well as can be expected," Steven said carefully. "They've made him comfortable. And, sir, that windbreaker of his. It's reversible. The other side's what they call faded jean blue."

Peacock grimaced. "That's handy."

They both looked casually towards the wreck, were startled to see Heath lash out feebly at Inspector Blaney who was leaning towards him. They heard his scream of pain—"No! No!", high pitched and anguished.

Peacock leaped at Blaney, spun him around, away from the wreck. "What the hell d'you think you're doing?" he snarled at the Auckland man.

"Nothing," said Blaney dabbing at his cheek. "I was just talking to him."

Steven bent over Heath. He was quiet now, too quiet. Eyes closed, face grey, blood trickling from the corner of his mouth, frothy blood which meant a broken rib had penetrated the lung.

"Just talking, eh?" grated Peacock. "And he tries to clock you one."

"Yes," said Blaney firmly. "I was just talking. I told him the truth. And he didn't like it. That's all!"

"The truth?"

"About his son's death. I told him the whole thing. I told him how we chased the Rebels into the Waitakaris. I told him how we surrounded the bach. And used loudhailers, to coax them out. I told him Scuddy must've realized it was hopeless, tried to make a break for it. And his cobbers, his great friends, shot him in the back. Kept on shooting at him when he fell. I told him how we broke in at the rear while the gang was occupied shooting at Scuddy. I told him about the inquiry, about police arms being handed in immediately. I told him all that. He, well, he kind of blew up. Couldn't take the truth, I guess."

"I see," said Peacock heavily. He might have said more but the ambulance arrived with the fire truck close behind. Steven felt a light touch on his hand, looked down at Heath, at the wild eyes, contorted mouth.

"Is it true?" gasped Heath.

189

"Yes," said Steven. "It's true. The police never even fired a shot."

"Oh, God! What have I done!" moaned Heath. He shuddered once, lapsed back into unconsciousness. Steven moved aside for the doctor who attended to Heath then signalled the firemen to start cutting.

Peacock asked, "D'you think he'll make it?"

The doctor shrugged. "Yeh. He'll make it. Nothing we can't put right. He'll hurt some for a while but he's okay. Take it from me."

Peacock turned a relieved face to Blaney. "Well, that's all right then. Sorry if I bawled you out. I thought—I thought—well, you could've killed him!"

"Yes," said Blaney quietly. "I could have."